Two Lights in War

Children of Aggressor Nations

Simon Miller

Published by Marianne Tong, aka Simon Miller, May 2016

War

When war crushes mankind's best intentions
And hate has set the world afire
Can any spark escape
To burn as love's desire?

Societies change and structures fall
Children of love must suffer much
While parents are absent,
They crave a loving touch.

Out of the ashes of destruction
The Phoenix rises yet again.
He looks around, sees naught but death.
God offers love. Accepting, he asks, when?

At a museum

"Hey Gramps, how many Noxies have you killed?"

A disrespectful teenager had approached a very old man sitting on a bench in a gallery of World War II pictures. The old man looked at the mouthy boy in surprise. He hadn't thought of himself as a killer. He had fought for his country.

"What makes you ask me such a rude question, young man?"

"I'm part of that group over there. Our history teacher brought us here to see pictures of World War II. I think it's all just a bunch of bull."

"A bunch of bull?"

"Yeah, people been killin' each other forever. What's so big about that?"

The old man had often wondered that himself. Now and then he came to the museum to reflect on his own history. Libraries filled with books about wars, museums filled with pictures of air planes, tanks, and other weapons, and the Internet filled with film footage of war scenes were all around to remind people of the horrors of war, and yet war keeps happening. He was not proud of his part in wars, but it was part of his life. And young people are asking question. What could he possibly tell them?

"You'd better get back to your group. Your teacher is probably looking for you."

"You a veteran?"

"Yes, I fought in World War II and the Korean Conflict. Hurry up, your group is leaving this gallery."

"We're s'pposed to interview a veteran. Lemme go ask my teacher if I can interview you."

Moments later the teen returned and sat down next to the old man. "My teacher said it was okay to talk to you for about fifteen minutes."

"Ha, ha. What can I possibly tell you in fifteen minutes about my ninety-two years of life?"

"Well, for starters you could tell me your name and phone number. That way I could call you to ask questions about stuff I need for the interview."

"Just call me Joe. Yeah, that'll do. GI Joe."

“Hey Gramps, you’re a funny old man. Okay, GI Joe it is. Lemme add your contact in my cell.”

“That’s a mighty fancy gadget. I’ll tell you what. If you teach me how to use a fancy thing like that I’ll tell you the story of a couple of little kids that lived during the same time that some truly terrible wars were happening.”

“Deal. My name is Randy.”

Shortly, GI Joe was telling Randy about two families on opposite sides of the war and the world.

“Randy, Everyone living today has been affected by World War II in one way or another. Even today, our peace and comfort is shakier than many of us realize. I can tell you stories about two families from opposite sides of the world, and how they coped. That may shed some light on why it’s important to learn about history.”

“Okay, I’m listening.”

“In Los Angeles, a Chinese grocer/butcher was raising a family of four sons. He didn’t know whether any of his boys would grow up to serve the gods of war or die trying. In Germany, a young father was drafted into the army, leaving his wife and very young daughter to fend for themselves during very hard times. That young father didn’t know whether his little girl would survive or die in the war.”

“Well, did they?”

“It’s a long story. They didn’t die; instead, they became points of light in the darkness of war. Eventually, because of the war, one of the boys met the little girl. Over the years they got married and even created a wonderful family."

"Will you tell me how that happened? We have to write an essay about how war affects survivors for history class, and I could ask my teacher whether I could write about your stories."

"I'd be happy to. Just call me on that fancy gadget of yours, and we'll set some time to meet in this very museum or in the library to talk about some of the good things that can come out of wars."

"Okay, but you never did tell me how many Noxies you killed."

"I honestly don't know. You see, I was a bombardier on a B-17. That's one of the airplanes that dropped a lot of bombs on German cities."

"On cities?"

"Yes." GI Joe's face had become very sad. He took a few moments to regain his composure. "At the time I really didn't think about the families with little children that lived there. I was just fighting the Nazis for my country."

"Nazis? I thought it was Noxies."

"Nazi stands for Nationalsozialistische Partei. That's the political party started by Hitler."

"Oh."

"You'd better run along now. Call me when you're ready to talk some more about wars and stuff."

"I will. Thanks Gramps, uh, I mean Joe."

* * *

A few days later, Randy called Joe. “Hey, remember me?”

“Sure.”

“Joe, I’m ready to start writing that essay. What can you tell me about those two little kids you were talking about the other day?”

“Well, Randy, Let me tell you a little about the parents of the little girl, and then I’ll tell you about the little boy. Be sure to take notes because I don’t want to repeat anything.”

“Are you going to tell me about the little girl, too?”

“Not today. You can call me again tomorrow. Ok?”

“Yeah, I’ll do that.”

Marianne's Parents

1939

In Koblenz, Germany, a young couple was arguing.

"Why do you have to join the Nazi Party? They are just a bunch of trouble-makers," yelled Tilly.

"If I want to keep my job with my insurance company, I have to register as a Nazi," shouted Jakob.

"What do the Nazis have to do with your job?"

"The Nazis are the government power now, and they are the ones who issue work permits. Only members of the party can get work permits. Even private companies, like the insurance company I work for, have to obey the law. They can only employ workers with work permits. My supervisor told me that they would have to let me go if I refused to join the party."

The young mother stopped arguing and hugged her young daughter. “Don’t worry Liebchen, your Mutti and Vati will do whatever we can to keep you safe.”

So Jakob signed up and continued to work with his company to provide a comfortable home for his little family until his draft notice arrived.

Leighton
1940

The four little boys sat stiff-backed on the hard wooden bench where their dad had put them. After what seemed like hours, Leighton, sitting next to Allen, the oldest who was pouting, got the nerve to ask no one in particular, "Why do we have to sit here so long?"

Jack, their father responded rather sternly, "We're waiting for your mom. The nurse will bring her out soon."

The youngest, only three years old, was getting antsy. "I want Mommy!"

Their father Jack was also getting anxious. Less than two months after their fifth child had been born, he was forced to take his wife back to the doctor. Something was wrong. She was acting strangely around the children. The doctor recommended a brief stay in the State Mental Hospital. Today, after consulting with the doctor again, he had to tell Suey that she would be confined there for a much longer stay.

They were expecting her at any moment in the beautiful, spacious backyard of the modern facility. Flowers and greenery surrounded the benches and lawn chairs for visitors. A door suddenly opened, and a nurse escorted Suey Ping toward the little group. No smiles, no hugs. A chair was placed near them, and Suey sat down. Jack took each little boy to her to shake her hand before returning him to the uncomfortable bench. The awkward silence was finally broken by a conversation in Cantonese Chinese. The boys, sitting silently, heard their parents' words but did not understand. They had expected their father to bring their mother home, but now there was talk of her staying in the hospital. What about their baby sister? Where was little Emily? The confusion was palpable.

Over the next three years the boys became accustomed to a routine of Sunday visits to the hospital. There might be a little hand-holding and an occasional pat on the head, but their mother remained aloof, often staring over their heads rather than engaging them in play or affectionate conversation. Afterwards, Jack took his boys to visit their baby sister, Emily.

"Dad, why is Auntie Number Three going to take Emily away?" Leighton had overheard a conversation between his dad and this lady who never came to their home.

"You're old enough now to learn the truth, Leighton. The woman who is taking care of Emily is my sister-in-law. Before your mommy and I got married, I had another wife who died. She had a couple of sisters who also lived in Los Angeles. When your mom got sick and went to the hospital, Emily was only two months old. I couldn't take care of the baby, so I asked one of my sisters-in-law to take the baby to her house."

"Oh. But I heard you say something about going to China."

"Yes, Auntie Number Three wants to go for a visit. I gave her permission to take Emily because she is her godmother. Emily thinks that she is her mother. Auntie Kai Nyung is too busy with your younger brothers Gene and Jerry to take care of another baby, so I'm letting Auntie Number Three take Emily to China."

Leighton went to tell Allen, his older brother about this new development. "Did you know that Emily is going to China with Auntie Number Three?"

"No, but a baby is useless, anyway. You 'n' me, we can go to school or we can play with friends. We can take care of ourselves. Gene and Jerry can take care of themselves at Auntie Kai Nyung's, but a baby? No."

"I think they're only going for a visit. That's what Dad said. Maybe when they get back and Mom gets out of the hospital, we'll be a whole family again."

"Look, Leighton, I want our whole family to be together again, too, but I'm only a little boy like you. We can't do anything about it. Dad's working all the time, Mom's in the hospital, Gene and Jerry live with Kai Nyung, and baby Emily is going to China. So, I'm just going to mind my own business. I'll go to school and learn something. I think I want to play tennis when I grow up."

Leighton mocked him, "Yeah, you go play tennis, and where are you going to get the money to buy a tennis racket, little poor boy." Then he got serious, "I wish I knew what made Mommy so crazy. I remember when she loved us and acted just fine, Allen."

Allen thought about this for a while. He also remembered Mom before Auntie Choy Ping went away. "Maybe she got sad and mad when Auntie left."

"Auntie? Which auntie?"

Leighton, now seven years old, was only three when his mother's sister, Choy Ping, had moved back to China. Choy Ping and Suey Ping were two of eight siblings. They had been born in the California Bay Area but taken back to the ancestral village near Canton, China in 1916 to be raised and educated in the Chinese culture. Their father owned and operated the Fook Wah Tong Herbal shop in San Francisco but could no longer support his large family, so he decided they would be better off in the ancestral home in the small Chinese village. He sent his wife and six children to China. Suey Ping, Leighton's mother was the first one to return to America.

When Suey Ping, an attractive eighteen-year-old, appeared in March 1930 unannounced in the Herbal shop, her father decided that he would have to find a husband for her as soon as possible. There were too many men looking for easy women in San Francisco. Marriage to a decent man would protect her, so he found a widower in the Los Angeles Chinese community. Jack was a butcher working in a grocery store. In September 1930, Suey and Jack were married.

The following year, Suey's sister, Choy Ping, arrived in San Francisco. Worrying about the brothels in San Francisco, her father sent her to live with her sister Suey in Los Angeles. For five years, Choy Ping worked as a seamstress and also helped out when Suey Ping's babies started arriving. Just before the fourth child was born, Choy Ping moved back to China, leaving Suey Ping with a husband she didn't love. How could she possibly manage by herself in this miserable apartment on East 10th Street with three little boys and another one on the way?

"Allen, what Auntie are you talking about?"

"Don't you remember Auntie Choy Ping? Mommy cried when she left."

"No." Leighton's memory was blurred. He knew that there was a baby sister in China with Auntie Number Three and some younger brothers in Los Angeles with Auntie Kai Nyung, but he was truly confused. "It didn't help to move to an apartment on Temple Street, either. Maybe that's why Mommy had to go to a hospital," his young mind speculated out loud.

Jack interrupted the conversation, "You boys need to stop all this talk. It doesn't do any good for you to worry about things. Your mom is sick, and that's all you need to know."

"Dad, I don't remember Auntie Choy Ping, but I remember some women screaming about baby brother Gene." Leighton's mind had cleared a bit. "Why were they screaming?"

"Come here boys. I'll tell you about it," said Jack who usually had very little to say.

"Yeah, Dad. Is that when we went on a train?" asked Allen.

"Let me finish, or I won't tell you anything." Jack took a few drags on his cigarette. "Here is what happened. Auntie Choy Ping was living with us, but she had to move back to China, so we took her to San Francisco on a train."

"We?"

"Yes, your mom and you three boys. Gene was just a baby. Your mom wanted to visit her father anyway, so we decided to make it a family trip. We even stayed in a hotel for a couple of days. A friend of your mom's, Mrs. Wong, had brought some food, and the women were getting all involved in talking while they were getting ready to serve lunch. Somebody noticed that baby Gene was missing. You two helped look around the whole room. Ha ha, you even looked under the bed, Allen. And Leighton looked out the window. All the women started screaming when Leighton pointed out the window and said, 'Gene.' There he was on the fire escape, butt-naked."

The boys laughed. Leighton said, "Dad, I always thought that I dreamed that."

"No, it wasn't a dream. It really happened. After that, the women were a lot more careful about watching you three boys. When kids are so little, they can get into all kinds of mischief."

"Yeah, Dad, do you remember how I got this scar?" Allen pointed at his forehead.

"I remember," answered Leighton. "You got hit by a car. We were sitting on the curb waiting for the ice cream truck. All of a sudden you jumped up. I guess you were going to run across the street for something. Just then a car drove by and knocked you down. You got up and ran away. That was so funny!"

"Funny?" Jack squinted threateningly at Leighton.

"Well, I couldn't help but laugh when Allen got up and ran away. I ran after him. I guess I was glad he was okay. When I caught up with him, I noticed some blood coming out of a small hole on his forehead. I helped him wash it, and I put a Band-Aid on it. Allen said he was fine, so we never told you about it."

"What did the driver of the car do?"

"I don't know. He probably didn't even know that he hit Allen because we both ran away."

In a Library

"Hi Joe, I'm ready to hear the story about the little girl, so I thought we'd meet here."

"Good idea, Randy. We won't be bothering anybody in this separate study room, and you can take notes on that fancy phone of yours. I'm going to buy one like that next week. I hope I can learn all the stuff you know."

"Ha! I don't know nearly as much stuff as you know, Joe."

"So we both have a lot to learn. Right?"

"So tell me about the little girl."

Marianne

1943

Even the children of the Isolierstation (isolation ward) had been dragged or carried into the make-shift bomb shelter in the hospital basement. Against the unfinished brick wall, six-year-old Marianne sat shivering on a hard bench between a heavily bandaged woman and a nurse in a crisp white uniform. The terror was palpable as pain and fear gripped the pathetic group. Barely able to whisper, she asked the nurse, "Is it another air raid? Will my mommy be alright?"

"Yes. Be still now. It will be over soon, then we'll go back upstairs." Silently the nurse wondered whether the hospital would survive another bombing. Many upper floor windows had already been broken, and one of the walls had been badly damaged.

Through her pain and fear Marianne worried more about her beloved mother and grandparents than about herself. All she wanted was to go home. Oma, her grandmother, would know how to make her feel better.

Back upstairs Marianne drifted in and out of consciousness for an indefinite time. She was in a bed with tall rails. Several times a day someone came to give her another injection, bring food or take her temperature. Then her perceptions cleared slightly, and she noticed all the other children in cages like her own. There must have been twenty or thirty in that cavernous hall. She guessed that it was the dreaded "Isolierstation" because they were isolated from the outside world and other patients but not from each other. All types of diseases were represented: measles, polio, diphtheria, scarlet fever, and who knows what else. Somehow, Marianne had entered the world of children who had no hope, no future, and no contact with loving relatives.

There were lots of injections, bad dreams, terrifying screams (perhaps her own) and waves and waves of pain. Marianne's ears throbbed. She couldn't move her legs. She was not touched by loving hands but by rough pulling and tugging which left her weak and unable to breathe. The food she received was often inedible. She had been accustomed to tasty food at her grandparents' home, and now she was forced to look at a bowl of grayish oatmeal or some other concoction which was simply not acceptable to a sick child's stomach. Marianne couldn't force her throat to swallow the goop which was stuffed into her mouth, and she usually let it drop back out. She was punished with a scolding and sometimes a slap for this behavior because it messed up the bed linens and made more work for the staff.

The main staple on the menu for midday and evening meals was a disgusting mixture of potatoes and apples. These were cut into bite size pieces and boiled in water, making a sort of whitish mishmash that was then served in enamel bowls. Even though Marianne had always enjoyed boiled potatoes, and was especially fond of applesauce, her diseased little body recoiled at the taste of the two cooked together in this unseasoned witches' brew. She yearned for a change of diet. Worse yet, the same portion in progressively deteriorating condition was served several times in a row as punishment for her stubborn refusal to eat. The same bowl of "Himmel und Erde" (heaven and earth) was grudgingly served along with lectures about the shortage of food, ungrateful children, and other unkind words.

The symptoms which had delivered Marianne into the hands of these demons were gradually replaced by behavior problems. The constant chiding by the nurses convinced her that she had become ill on purpose and was now behaving badly just to make the lives of the nurses more difficult. Their attitudes and grumbling did nothing to make her think otherwise. They reluctantly responded to her plaintive requests and often ignored her when she had to go the bathroom. If she wet the bed she was punished with another scolding or the subtle agony of being threatened with death.

She had been admitted for scarlet fever, but soon contracted diphtheria. After she had also contracted a virulent case of measles and become deaf as a result, she was taken into a frighteningly bright place. It was some kind of laboratory or operating room. She was held in a seated position on the lap of a nurse, and a young man in a white coat approached. Marianne was absolutely terror-stricken and for good reason. Long needles were pushed into both her ears and the pain made her faint. When she awoke, she was on a different ward and her head was bandaged. The subsequent treatment was worse than anything that she had ever endured before. The bandages were removed regularly and a length of medicated gauze was pulled from her ears. Then something was stuffed back into them, and the throbbing would begin all over again.

Along with the routine torturous treatments, there were the periodic visits to the air-raid shelter in the basement of the hospital while the rest of the world played war. The atmosphere of total terror and hushed silence among the adults in the shelters did little to speed the healing process. Sitting in the dark silence, she had no idea what was happening outside of her own painful presence, nor did she care. Marianne retreated into her own mind to shut out the suffering. She became completely internal and probably autistic. No one and nothing existed for her except her own six-year-old pain-ridden person. She forgot her formerly happy family life and only occasionally thought coherently. The word "Schule" (school) drifted in and out of her consciousness as did other isolated words that had no relationship to her conscious state. She no longer had an appetite and her body began to deteriorate. Her arms and legs became very thin, and any food that was forced into her stomach usually came out in spasmodic bursts of vomit or diarrheal discharge. She was, without a doubt, dying.

The incident which finally forced the staff to release her back to her family occurred as a result of her soiling her bed.

Marianne became conscious of terrific stomach cramps and being roughly lifted out of the mess. For some reason she understood, despite her bandaged ears that had been declared “deaf,” one nurse telling another, "Why don't you wash her over here in the sink, at least it has hot water?"

But the offer was refused. The rough-handed nurse told Marianne, “You don’t deserve to be washed in warm water! You need to be taught a lesson about pooping in bed! You have been a bad girl!” The nurse, a rough giant of a woman, then filled a tub with ice cold water and immersed Marianne, scrubbed her, and threw her shivering back into bed. Marianne must have gone into shock because a doctor was called. He declared her beyond help. Not too long after that, a couple of nurses dressed her in her street clothes and half-carried-half-walked her out to the main lobby. They had called Marianne’s mother to come get her.

Marianne was shocked by the expression of horror on her mother's face. She whispered, or perhaps only thought, "Don't you remember me, Mutti?"

Her mother gently took her to her grandparents' home in a taxi. There was nothing left of the robust six-year-old girl who had left the apartment six weeks earlier with a fever and a sore throat. Marianne had become a totally deaf and partially blind little skeleton, but there was enough left of her to sense the warmth and unconditional tenderness of her mother and her grandparents. Despite the repeated air raids, the entire population of the apartment house made it its business to nurse her back to health. Warm smiles appeared in front of her eyes again. People who had practically no food for their own families brought appetizing morsels in the hope that Marianne would be tempted into eating. Little by little she regained her trust in people and her appetite. Little by little she regained her hearing and sight. Marianne learned to laugh again. Her laughter made people forget for a moment that bombs were falling all around them.

* * *

How could anyone expect a little girl who had just started school after surviving six weeks in a hospital and three months in convalescence at home to draw perfect circles in order to produce a slateful of cursive a's? Apparently Marianne expected this of herself. She was crying pitifully, and her mother tried hard to soothe her.

"Come here Marianne, let me help you," Mutti said as she reached for the slate. "Give me your Griffel. I'll write them for you." A griffel is like a pencil, except that it is made out of slate and sometimes screeches as it is drawn across the wood-framed slate writing surface. Paper and pencils were scarce during the war, so school children had to practice their alphabets on wooden-framed slates.

"But, Mutti, I'm supposed to do this homework myself!" she protested. "The other children already know how to write. I'll never learn to write like they do. I hate writing!"

"Marianne, you're only six years old. You already know how to read. In time, you'll learn how to write," Mutti tried to be patient, but Marianne was crying harder than before.

"I can't! I just can't!" she yelled as she ran into her room and threw herself on the bed.

Their Löhrrondell apartment in Koblenz was still intact. Her room was full of toys. It was her comfort zone. The air raids had already inflicted a great deal of damage on Koblenz, but the apartment buildings on the Löhrrondell had been spared. The entire population of Germany still believed that normal life, including going to school, would go on. Children were still expected to learn reading, writing and arithmetic.

Only three weeks later the schools closed. By that autumn in 1943 the air raids had become too frequent and intense, and many people had left the city to escape to safer country villages. Koblenz was effectively shutting down. Marianne's father, like all the other young men, had been drafted into the army. The family hadn't heard from him since his last furlough, so Marianne and her mother spent a lot of time in the grandparents' cozy apartment in Koblenz-Lützel. Oma and Opa lived about a half hour's walk away from the center of town, but their neighborhood was no safer than the rest of the city streets. They could even see a railroad station from the living room window, and they knew that train tracks, especially depots, were prime bombing targets.

In a Library

"Man, Joe, I had a nightmare about the stuff you told me about Marianne."

"Did you write any of the stuff down?"

"Yeah, a rough draft, but now I need to hear more about the little boy, or the teacher ain't gonna be satisfied."

"Ahem, Randy, I hope you use better language in your essay."

"Sure, but we're just talkin'. Right?"

"Right."

Leighton

1941

"Dad, Dad! Leighton fell off his bike! He's bleeding!" Allen ran yelling into the small neighborhood grocery store.

The boys' father was working at the butcher block table in the back of the store. The Japanese owner at the cash register casually pointed in his direction, "He back there."

"Come on, Dad! Hurry up! Leighton is bleeding. Is he going to die?"

"Show me where he is, Allen. We'll take care of him." Jack remained calm and quickly grabbed his open pack of cigarettes before getting up. "I'll be right back, Mr. Matsuyama," he shouted on his way out.

"Dad, what do you need those cigarettes for?"

"You'll see."

They walked hastily for two blocks past the neglected homes. It seemed that nothing had been done to repair the potholes in the road or provide the houses with a fresh coat of paint for some time. Allen tripped on the uneven, cracked sidewalk, but Jack kept him from falling. "Dad, Leighton was just riding along, and then he probably hit something to make him fall off the bike."

Jack wasn't interested how it happened. He was almost out of breath. "Is it much farther?"

"No, see him? He's right over there."

Holding one hand tightly over his chest, Leighton was hunched over next to his twisted bike.

"Let's see how bad it is, Lai."

"No, no. If I let go, I'll bleed to death. I'm scared." Seeing his dad, Leighton began to cry.

"Stop it! You're eight years old. Big boys don't cry! Now let me look at how bad it is."

Reluctantly, Leighton lifted his blood-stained shirt off the wound on the right side of his chest. Fresh blood oozed out of a four-inch slit. "See? I fell on top of the handlebars."

Jack took the pack of cigarettes out of his pocket.

"Dad! Do something! You don't need to smoke right now!" Allen and Leighton yelled almost in unison.

Jack smiled and began to crumble one of the cigarettes, catching the loose tobacco in his hand. "Do you really think I don't know what I'm doing, boys?"

The boys were fascinated as Jack began to pack the tobacco into the open slit. "This tobacco will draw out any poison that might have gotten into the wound. It will also stop the bleeding pretty soon. Then we'll go to the clinic and get a tetanus shot just to be sure."

"A shot? Do I really need a shot?" Leighton had composed himself and looked at his dad in a whole new light.

"Yes. I need you boys to stay healthy." Jack was firm. "I need you to go to school and help me with your younger brothers and stock shelves in the store."

Leighton spent most of his summer vacation that year trying to repair his bike. He sat in the back yard of the duplex they shared with a neighbor, looking miserably at the ruined bike. The frame was fortunately still in pretty good condition. Even without the proper tools, he had been able to straighten the seat and repair the chain, but the front wheel was too warped to be of any use. He had gone to the used bicycle shop on the next block to scrounge bits and pieces, such as some grips for the handlebar, from the friendly owner, but a wheel was going to cost actual money. Leighton looked around unhappily. "*How am I going to get money to buy a wheel? Dad never gives me money for working in the store*," he thought. "*He lets me have an apple or some candy once in a while, but that's all.*"

Suddenly Leighton noticed some empty glass bottles near the neighbor's back door. "*I wonder how much I could redeem those for*." His mood brightened. "*I could probably buy a wheel that's still good!*" He went inside to get a cardboard box. Soon he was on his way with a box full of empty bottles to Mr. Matsuyama's store where his dad worked.

"Where did you get those bottles, Lai?" Mr. Matsuyama was suspicious.

"I've been collecting them around the neighborhood. Some people threw them away."

Jack looked at his innocent-looking young son and then told Mr. Matsuyama, who was busy at the cash register, "Please let him have the money for these bottles." Then he went back to his task of tending to the side of beef that had just arrived, mumbling, "I should take care of this meat and get it into the freezer before it spoils."

Leighton cheerfully skipped out of the store with a handful of coins.

The owner of "Woo's Used Bikes" checked the money. "Boy, you don't have much here, but you're in luck. I just happen to have a used wheel in the back for exactly that much money. It'll probably fit on your bike. All it needs is some air. Is the bike almost ready to ride?"

"Thanks, Mr. Woo. Yes, I got it all fixed up and all it needs now is a front wheel."

Mr. Woo smiled at the boy. "You sure have been working on that bike for a long time. Where did you get the money?"

"Collecting glass bottles."

"Well, here you go. Let's pump up the tire, and then you can take it home."

Soon Leighton was riding up and down the street, carefully avoiding the potholes. He didn't even notice the police car that was parked in front of the neighbor's house, and rode right past it. He rode around several blocks before he went back to get an apple from his dad's grocery store.

As he was getting close to the store, he heard his dad's firm voice calling, "Lai, you come here."

"*Uh oh*!" thought Leighton. "*What does he want me for? It's not my day to stock shelves.*" He got off his bike and went to see his dad who was talking to a couple of policemen.

"These policemen have been asking whether anybody had redeemed some glass bottles in our store. Our neighbors said that somebody stole their bottles right out of their backyard. The police even went to other stores like Woo's Used Bikes to investigate. I told them yes, that my very own son had redeemed some bottles. What do you have to say about that?"

Leighton nervously looked at his dad and at the two police officers who seemed to fill up the store. "Dad?"

"I'm ashamed of you boy!" He waggled his hand toward the officers. "Go ahead and take him."

"Dad! Those bottles were just sitting outside. I didn't...."

"Take him!"

Leighton felt very much alone in the holding cell at the neighborhood police station. He thought of his mother sitting alone in the hospital. Allen, his older brother was off somewhere playing with friends, and his brothers Gene and Jerry were at Auntie Kay Nyung's house probably getting something good to eat. "I'm hungry!" he told an officer who walked by.

"Sorry, we don't feed prisoners here at the station. You'll have to wait till they put you in a real jail."

Leighton panicked. "What will happen to me?" Another hour passed, and the little boy got more and more frightened.

Suddenly, he heard his dad's voice. "I'm ready to pick him up." A big feeling of relief washed over Leighton, and he tried to tell his dad, "I'm sorry."

Jack dismissed him. "I'm going to sell your bike, Lai, and then you will give the money to the neighbor and apologize. I hope you have learned a lesson. Let's go home. Dinner is waiting. Tomorrow we're visiting your mother."

* * *

Thoroughly chastised, Leighton followed him home to the Belmont Street Duplex. He looked at the spot where the bottles had been. "Man, I'm not going to collect bottles anymore."

The next day it was Leighton's turn to do the laundry. Allen and he had become quite adept at doing the household chores since their mother had gone away. The wringer washer, however, was a bit daunting.

"Darn this machine!" Leighton yelled as his wrist got caught between the rollers. He quickly hit the emergency release, and the rollers separated. He inspected his wrinkled skin and quickly shrugged off the pain. "*I wonder if this is more punishment for taking those stupid bottles.*"

No one was there to answer, so he kept struggling with the machine. After a while the laundry got done. Now all he had to do was hang wet clothes up to dry in the backyard.

All that work made him hungry. "*I wonder if there's anything left over from yesterday in the ice box.*"

Nothing. Leighton cooked a small pot of rice and cut up some Lahp Cheong (a Chinese sausage). A bit of soy sauce, and lunch was served!

After he cleaned up the kitchen, he left the house to see whether any of his friends could play. Maybe somebody could even go to Echo Park with him.

In the Library

"Hi Randy, are you ready for the next chapter?"

"Yeah. That story about Leighton was interesting, but it didn't have much to do with the war. I'm more curious about the little girl and all that bombing. How did they survive?"

"Patience, Randy. You'll find out in good time how Leighton was affected by the war. I'll tell you about Marianne, but first you need to look up a place called St. Wolfgang in Austria on that fancy phone of yours."

"Why?"

"It's a wonderful resort town now, but during World War II it was a sanctuary for wounded Allied soldiers, and there was a work camp for prisoners of the Dachau KZ Lager."

"Stop throwing those strange words around, Joe. What are you talking about?"

“Before and during the war, the Nazis had built a number of Concentration camps where they imprisoned anybody who spoke up against them. You probably already learned what they did to the Jews. Well, a lot of Germans who tried to defend or protect the Jews were also sent to these camps. They supposedly went to work in work camps, but many of them died while they were there.”

“Dang!”

“One of those work camps was near St. Wolfgang. Also, there were lots of fancy hotels in St. Wolfgang for wealthy European vacationers. The Allied forces took over those hotels and made them into hospitals for wounded soldiers. I’ll tell you about Marianne’s experience as soon as you’ve located it on a map.”

“Here, I got it! Nice!”

“Yes, it was nice before the war, and it is nice now, but during the war? Not so much.”

Marianne

1944-1945

"Listen, I think I hear an airplane," Tilly's ears perked up.

"No, if that were an airplane, the sirens would go off," Oma argued.

Moments later a loud boom surprised them both. "What was that?" They both jumped up so quickly, a cup of coffee hit the floor.

Opa came into the kitchen where Tilly and Oma were staring at each other in fear instead of enjoying their afternoon snack.

"I don't know, but now it's quiet again. If it was an airplane it was only one, not like the squadrons that usually …" Tilly was interrupted by the scream of sirens. Oma, Mutti and Marianne immediately grabbed their emergency bags and headed for the cellar that served as a makeshift bomb shelter. Every apartment house basement had been converted into a bomb shelter, but many people were killed when an entire apartment house collapsed on top of them. Yet, it seemed safer than remaining in a second or third floor apartment with windows that could send shards into a room. Opa quickly grabbed his volunteer fireman equipment and headed outside to participate in the civil patrol.

A half hour later they wearily and warily climbed the stairs back to the cake and coffee still waiting on the kitchen table.

“I’m so tired of this constant back and forth,” Oma declared. “I’m not going into a shelter anymore! From now on I’ll stay right here “If a bomb drops on me, it’ll be a quick death.”

Tilly shook her head, “You’re crazy, Mother! What would I do without you? I don’t want you to die.” She started to cry, so Marianne ran over to her and tried to wipe her tears away.

“Mutti, don’t cry. Let’s go home. I want to play with my dolls in my room,” she was begging selfishly.

“Marianne, as soon as Opa comes back he’ll tell us how the city looks after today’s air raid. Then we’ll go back to our Löhrrondell apartment, and you can play with your dolls.” Mutti assured her.

A couple of hours later, Opa reappeared. His face was grim. “Tilly,” he mumbled, “I have some bad news for you.”

“What happened? How bad is it?” Marianne could feel her mother trembling. “Marianne and I were planning to go home and spend the night there.”

“Don’t take Marianne. You can go look, but your apartment building is gone. The single airplane that flew over just before the air raid apparently released a couple of air mines over the Löhrrondell. The whole block is totally destroyed. The air raid kept us from getting close, but I saw it with my own eyes. It's nothing but a pile of smoking rubble now." Opa was trying to illustrate the destruction with gestures while Oma was slamming pots and pans around.

"I am so disgusted with this damned war! When is it going to stop! I've survived the war that was supposed to stop all wars when my children were babies! I've survived the ridiculous Inflation when money was worth nothing! I've kept my family alive through thick and thin, and I'm tired of this whole political crap that destroys more and more!" Marianne had never seen her grandmother so animated and so angry. Opa yelled something about Germany winning the war eventually.

"Vatter, do you think there's anything left to salvage?" Tilly interrupted their loud voices arguing about the war.

"There's no use. The whole block is completely destroyed. It's a good thing that you already took a truckload of your best furniture to your friends in Müden," he replied. Müden was a small village on the Mosel River about twenty-five kilometers away from the city of Koblenz. Against her husband Jakob's wishes, Tilly had transported her most valuable possessions to Müden for safe-keeping. Jakob had argued that the German government's promised insurance program would replace any losses sustained by the civilian population after the victorious end of the war. Tilly had remained skeptical. She wasn't so sure that Germany would win the war, so she had arranged to move some of her stuff. Now the rest was gone!

Marianne cried, "I'll never get to see my dolls again."

* * *

"I simply can't stay here anymore," Tilly wailed not too long after that fateful day. "Mother, have you ever heard of St. Wolfgang, a resort village in Austria?" Oma nodded. "The Allies have taken over all the hotels in St. Wolfgang for wounded British, American, French and Russian soldiers, so there's no bombing there. But no Germans are allowed into the village unless they have a local sponsor. Yesterday my friend Lotte got a letter, dated almost three weeks earlier, from her distant relatives who live in St. Wolfgang that they would sponsor us. So I'm taking Marianne, and we'll be leaving soon. She'll be able to go to school and learn how to write."

Oma was speechless. She had no idea that Tilly and her friend had been planning to escape. Tilly was resolute; she was not staying in Koblenz even if she had to walk away.

"You mean I'll be able to go to school in St. Wolfgang?" Marianne interrupted.

"Probably, Marianne. Come with us, Mother," Tilly was begging now.

"No, I'm not going to some strange village in the Alps. I'm so tired of this constant back and forth," the older woman declared again. "I survived the First World War in this apartment, and I survived the stupid Inflation imposed on us, and I'm planning to survive this mess Hitler has gotten us into. I'm not even going into a shelter anymore! From now on I'll stay right here," and she pointed at her pride and joy, her sparkling kitchen. "If a bomb drops on me, it'll be a quick death, and if no bomb drops on me, you'll have something good to eat when you return from the bomb shelter. I'm not leaving my home!"

The young woman shook her head, "Mother, please don't talk like that."

* * *

Shivering from cold and terror, two little girls huddled together on one of the twelve pieces of shabby luggage. The air-raids and bombings in the city of Koblenz had become unbearable. The pathetic little group, hoping to escape the bombs, included two fearful young women, Tilly and Lotte, and their two vulnerable daughters Marianne and Helga. Marianne, at age seven was the older one. Her experience in the hospital a year earlier had also made her terribly mature. Despite her own discomfort, she comforted Helga and tried to calm her mother who was fretting about the train arriving before the next air raid on this dark night.

"Mutti, the train will come, and then we'll be alright. Weine doch nicht! Don't cry!"

"Marianne, I'm crying because Oma and Opa didn't want to come with us. I'm worried that they will get killed in their own apartment in one of those horrible air raids."

"Now you're scaring me, Mutti. Let's go back and stay to take care of Oma and Opa. I love them."

"No, I've made up my mind. I can't stay in this city another minute."

The platform at the train station was crowded with lots of other escaping people. Surrounded by their bagged-up worldly goods, they were all hoping to find a place to survive the violence of this war. It was late October 1944, and the city had already sustained enough damage to convince the civilians that Germany would not be victorious. Even as a seven-year-old, Marianne vaguely understood the concept that simple personal survival had become more important than national pride.

Just when the sirens screamed their terrifying warning that more bombs were on the way, a freight train pulled into the station.

Not caring where the train was headed, all the waiting people clambered on. Some people were lucky enough to find an open cattle car where they could share space with some cows. Others had to climb onto the tops of the coal cars. Children and baggage were handed up. Gratefully, Marianne's little group of four found a place on top of the black lumps as the train carried them out of the city just as the bombs started to fall.

Throughout the night they traveled on. No lights anywhere. Occasionally the train stopped to avoid an air-raid in a near-by city. At each stop a few people got off to relieve themselves, but even more people climbed on to head south. The goal was Austria where the Alps would afford some shelter. Getting there was fraught with great danger.

"Mutti, I have to make peepee." Helga, Tante Lotte's five-year-old daughter whined.

"You have to hold it till the train stops again."

"I have to go too," added Marianne.

Tilly felt sorry for the little girls. "I know this is very hard, but we'll be in St. Wolfgang soon," she promised. "I won't get mad if you wet your pants."

When the train made one of its frequent stops in the dark of night, many people jumped off to relieve themselves under some nearby trees. Suddenly someone yelled, "Mach schnell!" (Hurry up!) "The train is moving again!" Everybody scrambled back on just in time. What a panic!

"Mutti, look over there. Lots of buildings are on fire."

"That's Würzburg, or maybe Regensburg. They must have had a terrible fire-bombing there."

They saw many such fires as they passed by cities and town. The little girls were terrified.

"Marianne and Helga, as long as the train tracks aren't damaged, we will be alright and keep on moving. We'll get to St. Wolfgang soon."

For three days and nights the little group traveled south. The little girls staunchly endured the stinging eyes from the coal dust and the discomfort from hunger, thirst and exhaustion. The two young women lived on the promise of better days. They were determined young mothers who would stop at nothing to protect their daughters.

* * *

"We are here. This is St. Wolfgang," Tilly announced one afternoon. "Let's get off this terrible coal car. Marianne looked around even though her eyes were stinging from the coal dust. Snow, great mountains and a huge lake made the world seem very bright. She was reminded of scenes described in her favorite book, *Heidi,* but the cold had become too insistent for reflection. She and Helga shivered as the luggage was handed down. The train left, and there they stood. Where was the town? "Mutti, I don't see any houses. I'm cold and hungry. Where are we going to sleep and eat?"

"We will have to wait for the ferry to cross the lake. It's the only way to get to the town. Look! Way over there! On the other side of the lake. That is St. Wolfgang. See, there is a church! And, see? The ferry is on its way."

Marianne was sure she didn't want to make that trip across the ice-cold water, but to please her mother, she bravely joined the crowd boarding the rickety raft. Helga followed. Where was the motor? "Hold on to your baggage, folks. We're not fishing anything or anyone out," one of the ferrymen grumbled. Marianne checked her backpack. Everyone had several pieces of luggage to take care of. Even Helga had to wear a backpack and carry two small suitcases. A loud creaky sound announced that the ferry had left the shore. Four strong ferrymen rowed the ferry toward the town while the passengers remained as quiet as possible.

Once she felt the solid ground of the village under her feet, Marianne began to chatter incessantly. "Where are we going to sleep, when are we going to eat? I need to pee. Will I be able to go to school here?"

Her mother patiently explained, "Calm down. We will be staying with some relatives of Tante Lotte. They sponsored us, and they know we're arriving today."

When the bedraggled group of four refugees arrived at their small home, Lotte's cousin and her husband were not too pleased. They grudgingly shared their food. They were not very friendly. Tilly and Lotte agreed that the family probably resented four extra mouths to feed in their home. They would have to find another place to live right away.

St. Wolfgang had been a resort town during better times. There were fifteen fancy hotels, numerous restaurants and a number of "Pensions" which are typical bed and breakfast boarding houses. Before the war, vacationers had enjoyed skiing during the winter seasons and water sports during the summers. Traces of the happy years were everywhere; however World War II had changed the character of this place.

Now St. Wolfgang had become a sanctuary for the Allies. The fifteen hotels served as field hospitals. The wounded military being cared for included Americans, English, French soldiers as well as some German prisoners of war. One sub-camp of the Dachau concentration camps was located in a valley just outside of town. A general agreement among the Allies had made the airspace above St. Wolfgang a "no-fly" zone. No bombs would be dropped there. Entry into this town was strictly controlled, and only those who were sponsored by local people were allowed to enter. Tilly and Lotte had to consider themselves lucky, but they certainly didn't feel lucky. They felt unwelcome and lost.

Finally, the two young women found a couple of rooms in a summer boarding house. The windows were single panes, and one free-standing ceramic coal heater was expected to provide comfort on cooler summer nights. Unfortunately, the building had not been built for family occupancy during the harsh Alpine winters. There was no kitchen, no running water, and no private bathroom. A well in the yard provided the water. A common necessary facility was located down the hall halfway down the stairwell; however, Tilly's resourcefulness and talents soon transformed this temporary shelter into a cozy home.

Tilly offered her expertise in dress-making to anyone she met. She had done her apprenticeship with a master tailor for three years after finishing school at the age of fourteen. In Koblenz, her dress-making skills had provided additional income for her family for years. In better times, she had even sewn all the dresses for her own wedding party. Now her skills were particularly practical because store-bought clothes were unavailable.

The owner of a St. Wolfgang restaurant hired her to do her sewing and mending in exchange for one daily meal for all of them. This arrangement proved to be very satisfactory. After months of hunger, they were eating a hot meal every day. Best of all, they didn't have to worry about bombs dropping into their soup! Lotte also found a job. She became a housekeeper for a local St. Wolfgang family.

The four refugees began to feel comfortable in this unfamiliar town, however, it was difficult to overcome old habits. One time, when taking a Sunday afternoon stroll, Marianne and her mother heard some airplanes approaching. They hid under a sturdy park bench to avoid being strafed. Onlookers laughed. They tried to assure the young woman that no harm would come to her here. It took a while for them to accept a normal routine.

"Mutti, I want to go back to Oma's house," Marianne declared one morning after a particularly difficult night of fearful dreams.

"Marianne, Koblenz has become too dangerous. I got a letter from Oma yesterday. She says that the air raids and bombings are going on all day and night. We can't go back. We have to stay in St. Wolfgang until the war is over," her mother's voice soothed her despite the fearsome information it conveyed.

"If we have to stay, why can't I go to school here?"

"I promise, tomorrow I'll go to the school to see whether you can be in the second grade. They might put you in first grade because you didn't go to school in Koblenz for the whole first grade."

"But I can read, and Opa taught me how to do math."

"Yes, I know that you are smart enough for second grade, but rules are rules."

School proved to be a troublesome thought. By age seven Marianne should have been in the second grade. Measured by her reading skills she could have been in the fourth grade, but by her writing skills she was nowhere. What would the teacher think? How would the other students treat her? She was very apprehensive but eager to try going to school.

"You'll start tomorrow morning," Tilly announced a week later. "First I have to buy you a new slate, a couple of Griffels, those hated slate styluses, and a sponge for erasing, and then I'll take you to school."

"I'm scared, Mutti, can't you stay there with me?" after she looked into the classroom she wasn't at all sure she wanted to go to school after all. "Maybe I don't have to go."

"You were constantly begging me to let you go to school. What happened?" Tilly was puzzled about her new attitude.

"It's so dark and cold in that classroom. And I don't know anybody. And the teacher looks scary. And…"

"Stop! You're going, and that's that!" Tilly ended the discussion.

For two weeks Marianne sat miserably in the cold, light- and lifeless classroom, not understanding what was going on. No one paid particular attention to her, so she did her best copying things from the blackboard and generally making a mess out of her slate. Her handwriting did not improve, and she had to make frequent use of the grubby little sponge that had taken on an unpleasant odor in its moist canister.

"Well, Marianne, you are getting your wish. You don't have to go to school anymore."

Marianne was puzzled. She thought, "*Mutti usually doesn't give in to me. I wonder what happened. Did the teacher throw me out?*" She asked, "Why not?"

"Your teacher and several others have been arrested. Nobody has told me what they did, but I think it has something do with being Nazis," Tilly explained. "Maybe he was a spy, or whatever. I'm not even sure who arrested him, the Allies or the Nazis. All I know is that the second grade does not have a teacher anymore. There are only a few teachers left for some of the older students. The rest of the younger kids have to stay home."

"Yay! I get to play with Helga all day," Marianne was elated. "I don't have to sit in that horrible room anymore!"

"Yes, but there better not be a lot fighting. Tante Lotte and I are nervous enough without you two little devils screaming at each other about every little thing," her mother's face was stern. She had a lot to worry about, and her nerves were already at a breaking point without Helga and Marianne bickering about the most insignificant things.

"We'll be good," Marianne promised, but she was already eyeing Helga with a mischievous smirk. "*I'm older and bigger, and Helga will have to do what I want*," she thought gleefully as she scampered away.

As the winter grew more severe, new problems entered their lives. Food had become scarce even in the restaurant, and the water pump in the front yard was frozen solid. Fuel for the heater was rationed and delivered each month. One cord of firewood per household was supposed to last for a whole month.

It got so cold that the pillows on the beds had thin layers of ice. "Mutti, I don't like this cold pillow. Why is there ice on it?"

"Marianne, the moisture from your breath made the pillow a little wet. It got so cold that the moisture froze. Let's shake it for a little while to break off the ice."

“I have a good idea, Mutti. Let’s sit on the pillow for a while. Our butts will warm them up.”

“Ha ha, let’s try that.”

Despite the hardships, Tilly and Lotte were preoccupied with making Christmas a happy time for the two little girls.

From a local carpenter, Tilly purchased a wheeled pull-toy with several spindles that turned on a platform. When she made a number of cute doll dresses from remnants and scraps, it was like magic. Presto! Dancing Dolls for Christmas. A little tree decorated with homemade ornaments, paper chains and cookies completed the festivities. The cookies tasted a little funny from the rancid butter Tilly was able to acquire, but the girls didn't mind. Marianne knew that, her mother had provided the most important ingredient: Love. The four refugees somehow gathered together and celebrated Christmas by singing "Stille Nacht." (Silent Night) Marianne was conscious of her mother's tears and felt her sadness. That night she prayed and prayed that her mother would be happy in the future.

In reality the future held more terrors. To avoid the poverty, Lotte did what she could to earn rent money. Tilly was desperately providing food and winter clothing for the group. When the news reached her ears that a supply of sugar and other staples had become available in Bad Ischl, she determined to go that neighboring town on the other side of the lake. Marianne begged her not to leave because she was terrified that she would have to cross the lake in the middle of winter. Tilly felt she had to try.

Marianne cried herself to sleep when her mother had not yet returned by midnight. She was sure that her mother had died. Early in the morning Tilly returned, nearly frozen to death. She had quite a story to tell.

“I had finished buying the sugar and a couple of other things in Bad Ischl. The train back to St. Wolfgang was delayed, but I decided to brave the late night return trip. When I, and one other lone passenger, got off the train, we realized that no ferry would be able to cross the lake. The lake had frozen solid while I was gone! The other passenger was a young man in uniform. Perhaps he was a soldier on furlough or a deserter. Who knows? Anyway, he set out across the frozen lake on foot. I was afraid to be left alone at the train station, so I followed him. I was loaded down with all these supplies and trudged along slowly. I begged him to walk a little slower, but he headed faster and faster toward the tiny lights shining through swirls of snow. However cold and poor the village was, it would be infinitely more comforting than the icy water under our feet. For more than an hour, I pressed on. Now and then the ice was covered with pools of water several inches high. One time I even stepped in a soft spot that allowed water to spill over the tops of my boots. My feet got wet, and they felt like ice. Believe me, Marianne, the icy fear that gripped my heart was worse than the ice below my feet.”

“Oh Mutti! I love you. Don’t go away anymore.”

For the next few weeks, they nursed Tilly back to health. Even Helga stopped screaming about every little thing. Tilly was strong. Soon she was back at the sewing machine inspiring the group toward better times with stories of personal triumph over impossible situations.

One such triumph arose out of a crime of desperation. The new ration of firewood had been stacked in the St. Wolfgang market place. Each household was assigned one cord of firewood in logs one meter long and about six inches in diameter. Hoping to increase their resources, Tilly and Lotte decided to help themselves to more wood. Stealthily they dragged several logs home in the dark of night. The next day when they went to pick up their legally allotted portion, they were told that someone had stolen their cord of wood. Despite a guilty conscience, Tilly was able to make such a scene that the supervisor felt sorry for her. She was given another cord of wood, all cut to the proper size for the stove. Her ill-gotten logs were never discovered, although it was extremely difficult to make use of them. The logs were too big for the space heater. With a tiny kitchen knife, she had to carve slivers that could be used as kindling, but at least she wasn't arrested for theft!

With love and a sense of humor the group somehow survived that terrible winter, and enjoyed the warming spring. News of the war brought new hopes and fears. There was a rumor that the Russians were advancing toward St. Wolfgang, raping every female in sight and killing anyone who offered the slightest resistance. They also heard of the Americans advancing from another direction, taking young women for sex and giving chocolate and cigarettes to children and old people. Nobody knew which army would reach them first. Tilly and Lotte prepared to escape within a moment's notice. Their luggage was all packed for days, ready to move out.

One sunny afternoon Marianne was playing in the yard. Suddenly a Jeep passed by the boarding house. It was American! She ran screaming upstairs, "Mutti, Mutti, come quick! The Americans are coming!" All the people in the boarding house poured into the street, breathing a collective sigh of relief. Soon a convoy of tanks, jeeps and large trucks with noisy flag-waving Americans who tossed chewing gum and Hershey chocolate bars to the children. The slow-moving joyous convoy moved past the house toward the town. The worst appeared to be over.

* * *

"Marianne, the war is over! We'll be able to go home soon."

Going back home to Koblenz proved to be as difficult as getting to St. Wolfgang. In the general hubbub of the American take-over and the warming of a spring June, Tilly became very ill. She had large boils in her mouth and was unable to eat. She grew weaker with each passing day. Once again Marianne was afraid for her mother's life. Just when all hope was gone, two men came to the rescue. Lotte's husband, Joseph, and Tilly's brother, Jupp, arrived to help get the family back to Koblenz. During the night, Tilly's fever broke and the boils got smaller. Despite Tilly's ill health, the group of six set out across the lake to the train station. Eventually they boarded a passing freight train.

Again, the return trip took three days and nights. In horror they spotted the devastated cities as the train slowly lumbered on. The passengers crowded in cattle cars or on top of coal cars held their breaths and stopped all talk whenever the train crossed one of the make-shift bridges which creaked under its weight. Now and then everyone had to walk and carry their luggage in order to transfer to another train where the tracks or a bridge had been destroyed and not yet repaired.

When the miserable little group arrived in Koblenz, friends and neighbors who had remained behind were shocked. Tilly, whose body was racked with the infection, was barely able to stand up. Marianne was fairly robust except for her eyes. The coal dust and other pollutants had caused them to generate a discharge which glued her eyelids shut. She had to use her fingers to pry her eyelids apart. Lotte and Helga were also emaciated and sick. The group needed fresh water, food, and medicine. Unfortunately, all of these were scarce in Koblenz. Even though Marianne's grandparents' apartment house was still standing, Oma and Opa had moved out. The city had been eighty percent destroyed. How could anyone survive?

Though the bombing had stopped, misery was everywhere. Many people who had lost their homes were looking for shelter. The authorities forced anyone who still had an apartment to share rooms. Oma's kitchen, was now occupied by another unfriendly family. The room that Tilly and her sister had shared while they were growing up was occupied by a stranger, and only the former master bedroom remained for the original family renter. With broken hearts, Oma and Opa had left their beloved home in the city and moved to Macken, the village where Oma was born. Uncle Jupp and a German girl he had met in Paris had made their home in the one remaining room, so there was not enough room for Tilly and Marianne to move into the apartment for more than a couple of days. Though they were home, they had not yet come home.

"Jupp, I think I'll try to take Marianne to Macken."

"That would be for the best, Tilly."

"Mutti, what is Macken?"

"That's the name of the Hunsrück village where Oma and Opa live now. It's only an hour away from Koblenz. I think they have room for us and food because the farmers live there. If the train still goes in that direction, we'll go visit them soon."

Just a couple of days later, Tilly took Marianne on another complicated train ride to visit her grandparents in the village. Tilly stayed just long enough in Macken to regain her health before leaving. She couldn't find work in the village, so she decided to return to Koblenz. Her plan was to look for her former clients who might be able to help her earn a living with her sewing skills.

* * *

A few months later Jakob, who had been taken prisoner of war, also returned to Koblenz. He was a broken man, unable to assume the duties of a husband and father.

Against all odds, Marianne's parents had managed to return to Koblenz, their hometown, which now lay in ruins. Would they be able to find a place to live, pull the family together and strive toward a better future?

In the Library

"Hi Randy, I was hoping you'd come back. I was beginning to think that these stories were boring you."

"No way, Joe. I'm putting together an essay that'll earn me an A."

"That would be nice."

"So Joe, let's talk about little Leighton. How did the war affect him in Los Angeles?"

Leighton
1942-1945

The crowded Chinese restaurant in Los Angeles was suddenly thrown into total darkness. A couple of startled women let out short screams, and then there was a lot of murmuring and shuffling of furniture.

"Dad, what happened?" Leighton wasn't exactly scared, but he and his brother Allen hadn't been prepared to sit quietly in a completely dark restaurant. No one even brought out a flashlight.

"Quiet, boys! This is a practice blackout."

"A practice blackout? What's that?"

"Just sit still, and I'll tell you. You'd better not get up. I want you to listen to me. This is important!"

"Dad, you're scaring me," said Allen.

“There’s good reason to be scared Allen. There’s a war going on.”

“A war?”

“Yes, last December, the Japanese air force flew all the way to Hawaii, and then they dropped bombs on Pearl Harbor. Several American ships that were anchored there got destroyed.”

“Why’d they do that, Dad?”

“I really don’t know. Sometimes a country attacks another country, and then that attacked country fights back. Before you know it, a war starts. It’s happened before throughout history. Right now, some very bad things are happening all over the world. People are fighting and killing each other, and they use terrible weapons.”

The boys were sitting in the darkness, absorbing their dad’s words while chairs and tables were being moved and people were staggering around.

“Shh! This blackout is just for practice in case the Japanese airplanes fly all the way to Los Angeles at night. When they don’t see any lights, they’ll think that there are no buildings, so they’ll fly someplace else to drop their bombs.” Jack was trying to make things easier for his young boys to understand. Instead he frightened them even more. “Now you’re really scaring me, Dad,” whispered Leighton.

“Not me!” yelled Allen. If they try to drop bombs on our house, I’ll kick their butts.”

Several people giggled at the boy’s bravado in the dark.

Suddenly the half empty restaurant lit up brightly again. “Dad, what happened to all the people?”

“I guess they got scared and ran away,” suggested Jack.

Allen smiled, “I guess they didn’t want to pay for their food.”

* * *

“From now on I want you boys to come to the store right after school,” announced Jack one day.

“But I practice tennis at Echo Park after school,” argued Allen.

“I need you to work at the store. If you do good work for two hours, you can go play your tennis.”

“I like working at the store, Dad,” offered Leighton. “Is Mr. Matsuyama going to pay me?”

“Mr. Matsuyama doesn’t own the store anymore, Lai.”

“Why not? Who owns it now?”

“Remember when I told you about the Japanese attacking Pearl Harbor?”

“Yes.”

“Well, now the President has decided to force all Japanese people living in America to sell their stores and houses. He’s making them move to special camps. Mr. Matsuyama got moved to Manzanar,” Jack explained. “He and his whole family are living there.”

Allen perked up. “Did Mr. Matsuyama give the store to somebody else? Who is going to be your new boss, Dad?”

“I’m buying the store.”

The boys were shocked. “You what?” They both looked at their dad who looked back at them. For a moment all three were quiet.

Leighton said, “I thought we were poor. Dad. How can you buy a whole store? How are you going to do that? We’re poor.”

“I’m going to borrow the money from a bank. Every month I will pay some money to the bank until all the money is paid back. If I can’t pay, the store will belong to the bank. That’s the way things are done.”

“Oh, I get it!”

“And that’s why I need you boys to help me out. I will be very busy with all the things that Mr. Matsuyama used to do while I took care of the butchering and keeping the shelves stocked. After he leaves, somebody will have to help me with the shelves and watch the cash register. When I’m busy with the paperwork or the butchering, one of you will have to be in the store to watch out for customers that might take something without paying.”

“Who’s going to help you while we’re at school?”

“Auntie Kai Nyung promised to help me while Gene and Jerry are at school. She’s been a trusted friend and Godmother for years, so I can trust her with the money.” Jack had been spending a lot of time at her house.

“Maybe Mom could leave the hospital and help you,” offered Leighton.

“No, your mother is not well. End of discussion. Just make sure you come directly to the store after school.”

“Yes, Dad.”

* * *

Working at the store was not so bad. Leighton still had plenty of time to visit friends. He was particularly fond of a young girl named Jacqueline. Her mother was always home, “Would you like some cookies and milk?”

"Yes, please."

"Mom, could we please use this old cardboard box," Jackie asked.

"What for?"

"Leighton and I want to slide down the hill behind our house."

"Sure, but don't mess up your school clothes."

One day, Leighton went to see Jackie. Everything in the house had been rearranged, and there were boxes everywhere. "What's happening, Jackie?"

"We're moving, so my parents are packing everything up."

"We move around a lot too. My dad is always trying to find a better apartment somewhere. We just moved to a new apartment behind our store. What street are you moving to?"

Jackie's face darkened a bit, "Leighton, we're leaving Los Angeles. We're moving to Washington."

"Washington, D.C.? The capital of America?"

"No, Silly! Washington State. My dad got a new job in Seattle."

"Oh."

On his way home, Leighton kicked the sidewalk a few times, but he soon found another friend, a black boy named Alex. Alex's family owned and operated the "Townsend Dry Cleaners" a few doors down from "Jack's Chinese Grocery."

"Hey, Alex, you want to go to Echo Park later? We could get some exercise on the equipment." There were Rings, Parallel Bars, High Bars and even some big Swings for the older kids.

"Yeah, let's go. My dad said not to fish in the lake, though. He doesn't want me to get in trouble with the law."

"Nah, don't worry. We'll just get some exercise before dinner," Leighton assured him.

When Alex invited him to come to church, Leighton agreed. He was a bit surprised that he was the only person who was not black, but he enjoyed the Baptist services anyway. "Would it be alright for me to come to church with you on Sundays?"

"I'll ask my mom," said Alex. Soon Leighton was attending regularly except for one Sunday a month, but he did not join the church officially.

* * *

"Leighton, do you know where Allen is?" Jack seemed annoyed. "I haven't seen him all day, and there's a lot of work to be done."

"I didn't see him after school, so I thought he was already here."

"Well, he's not. In fact, he gets out of working here every chance he gets."

Leighton knew that Allen had sneaked off to play tennis again, but he didn't say anything. Dad might take Allen's tennis rackets away. Allen was getting quite good at this sport, so Leighton covered for him.

"Don't worry, Dad. We'll get all the work done. I'm real good at stacking stuff on the shelves."

"Alright. When you see Allen, tell him that we're going to see Mom this Sunday. I want him there."

"Yes, Dad."

Once a month Jack took the two older boys to visit their mother in the Norwalk State Hospital. These visits were usually a big disappointment. While Jack and the boys eagerly waited on one of the benches on huge lawns surrounding the hospital, Suey Ping was escorted out to meet her family. It was difficult to tell what the smiles on her face meant. She seldom talked to the boys or gave them an affectionate hug; instead, she talked to Jack about no particular topic. Then the visit was over. The drive home was always subdued. Allen had not gone for three months. Leighton kept hoping that his mom would come home.

Jack grumbled something and went back to work, leaving Leighton wondering why he wasn't bringing Mom home. She seemed to be alright.

* * *

Jack feared that his two older sons, Allen and Leighton, were becoming too independent. Allen was spending far too much time playing tennis, and Leighton was always at some friend's house. He wondered briefly where they were getting the money to pay for their activities. They hadn't asked him for money for quite some time.

One early morning, Jack noticed a stack of newspapers on the front porch. "What's this?" he asked Leighton who was rubbing the sleep out of his eyes.

"I've got a newspaper route," he proudly explained.

"But you're only eleven years old. You need to get plenty of rest for school."

"Don't worry, Dad, I can take care of myself. I've been reading the headlines. America is winning the war. I've also been talking to a lot of soldiers."

"What? Where do you see soldiers? How do you get to talk to them?" Now Jack was beginning to wonder about his son.

"I shine their shoes."

Jack was speechless. Finally, he said, "Tell me about it."

"Sometimes I take the bus downtown to shine shoes."

"For money?"

"Yeah, I have a nice shoe shine kit, so I go downtown and sit near the bus stop. When I see a couple of soldiers getting off the bus, I ask them whether they would like their shoes shined up. Some of them laugh at me and tell me I'm too little, but I tell them I do a good job. Afterwards they give me a quarter."

"What do you do with that money, Lai?"

"I have to pay for my bus fare and shoe polish, but I have enough left over to go to the movies."

"Do they talk to you about the war?"

"Some soldiers like to talk and brag, but some of them just sit there while I'm shining their shoes. One of them even told me that he hoped I would never have to go to war. Dad, do you think I'll ever have to go to war?"

"I don't know, Lai. It's hard to think about an end to all the fighting. There's always going to be somebody who starts another fight. Maybe by the time you're old enough to put on a uniform, the United Nations will stop all the wars."

"The United Nations, Dad?"

"I heard President Roosevelt talking about that on the radio, but I don't really know anything about it. Maybe you can read about it in one of your newspapers."

"Dad, I don't really read them. I just deliver the newspapers and look at the headlines once in a while."

“Well, you’re still very young.”

Jack was proud of his son, but these discussions were rare. He especially avoided any discussion about his wife who was still in the State Hospital.

In the Library

"Hey Randy, long time no see. Did you get an A on that essay?"

"Yup, but now the teacher wants me to find out what happened to those two kids after the war. Are they still alive?"

"Are you going to write another essay?"

"Yeah, I been thinkin' about it. I kinda like getting' A's. I guess I'll try writing some more about these two kids. Besides, you got me curious now."

"Yes, Randy, they are still alive. I'm going to have to tell you some stuff about that time after World War II, or the story about the two kids won't make any sense. Are you ready to take notes?"

"Lay it on me, Joe."

Joe smiled. “Here goes.”

“More big words, Joe?”

“Yes.”

“Randy, have you ever learned anything about the Aftermath of World War II in Europe?”

“Well, just the other day, the teacher was talking about the Marshall Plan. He told us that millions of Germans had died and many millions more had become homeless. The German economy had collapsed, and much of the European industrial infrastructure had been destroyed. Even the Soviet Union, had been affected. In response, in 1947, U.S. Secretary of State George Marshall devised the "European Recovery Program", which became known as the Marshall Plan. Under the plan, during 1948-1952 the United States government allocated thirteen billion Dollars for the reconstruction of Western Europe. The teacher used the word ‘aftermath.’ Is that what you mean?”

“Exactly! Hey, you sound like an expert.”

“Well, I’m getting so involved in the history that I even surprise myself with how much I’ve learned.”

“How much do you know about the Allies splitting up Germany into occupation zones?”

Randy was proud to explain, “The Russians took East Germany and part of Berlin, and the Americans, the English and the French split up West Germany and the rest of Berlin. I heard that you had to have special passes to travel from one zone to another.”

Joe agreed, "Right. Have you learned anything about Denazification?"

"Nah, that's a new one on me."

"Better take lots of notes. This is going to take a while, but it's important in order to make sense out of the story of Leighton and Marianne."

"Okay."

Joe explained, "Denazification in Germany was attempted through a series of directives issued by the Allied Control Council, seated in Berlin, beginning in January 1946. "Denazification directives" identified specific people and groups and outlined judicial procedures and guidelines for handling them. Though all the occupying forces had agreed on the initiative, the methods used for denazification and the intensity with which they were applied differed between the occupation zones.

About 8.5 million Germans, or 10% of the population, had been members of the Nazi Party. Nazi-related organizations also had huge memberships, such as the German Labor Front (25 million), the National Socialists People's Welfare organization (17 million), the League of German Women, Hitler Youth, the Doctors' League, and others. It was through the Party and these organizations that the Nazi state was run, involving as many as 45 million Germans in total. In addition, Nazism found significant support among industrialists, who produced weapons or used slave labor, and large landowners, especially the Junkers in Prussia. Denazification after the surrender of

Germany was thus an enormous undertaking, fraught with many difficulties.

The first difficulty was the enormous number of Germans who might have to be first investigated, then penalized if found to have supported the Nazi state to an unacceptable degree. In the early months of denazification there was a great will to be utterly thorough, to investigate everyone and hold every supporter of Nazism to account; however, it turned out that the numbers simply made that goal impractical. It soon became evident, too, that pursuing denazification too scrupulously would make it impossible to create a functioning, democratic society in Germany, one that would be able to support itself economically and not become a burden on the victorious nations. Enforcing the strictest sanctions against lesser offenders would prevent too many talented people from participating in the reconstruction process. The Morgenthau Plan had recommended that the Allies create a post-war Germany with all its industrial capacity destroyed, reduced to a level of subsistence farming; however, that plan was soon abandoned as unrealistic and too likely, because of its punitiveness, to give rise to German anger and aggressiveness. As time went on, another consideration that moderated the denazification effort in the West was the concern to keep enough good will of the German population to prevent the growth of communism.

The denazification process was often completely disregarded by both the Soviets and the Western powers for German rocket scientists and other technical experts, who were taken out of Germany to work on projects in the victor's own country or simply seized in order to prevent the other side from taking them. The U.S. sent 785 scientists and engineers from Germany to the United States, some of whom formed the backbone of the U.S. space program.

In the case of the top-ranking Nazis, such as Göring, Hess, von Ribbentrop, Streicher, and Speer, the initial proposal by the British was to simply arrest them and shoot them, but that course of action was replaced by putting them on trial for war crimes at the Nuremberg Trials in order to publicize their crimes while demonstrating that the trials and the sentences were just, especially to the German people. However, the legal foundations of the trials were questioned, and the German people were not convinced that the trials were anything more than 'victors' justice."

Randy gasped, "Slow down, Joe!"

"What's the problem, Randy."

"I'm only a high school student, not a college professor. This is too many big words and too much information for me all at once."

"Sorry, I got carried away. I haven't even told you how they dealt with the money problem after the war."

"Oh man, I need to leave pretty soon. Can you make it short?"

“Sure. After the war, the Reichsmark continued to circulate in Germany, but with new banknotes (Allied Occupation Marks) printed in the US and in the Soviet Zone, as well as with coins (without swastikas). Actually, the Reichsmark was nearly worthless. For all intents and purposes, it was supplanted by a barter economy (commonly, "cigarette currency"). The Reichsmark was completely replaced in June 1948 by the Deutsche Mark in the Trizone (three western occupation zones) and (in the Soviet Occupation Zone) later in the same year by the Ostmark in East Germany. The 1948 currency reform under the direction of Ludwig Erhard is considered the beginning of the West German economic recovery; however, the secret plan to introduce the Deutsche Mark in the Trizone was formulated by economist Edward A. Tenenbaum of the US military government. He executed his plan abruptly on 21 June 1948. It took the German people by surprise. Three days later, the new currency also replaced the Reichsmark in the three Western sectors of Berlin.”

“Wow, Joe. It seems like the survivors of the war had a lot to deal with in the aftermath. I can hardly breathe just hearing about it.”

Joe smiled at the stunned boy, “Randy, remember there were also Jewish Casualties and Survivors.”

“Hey Joe, I’m almost afraid to ask ‘cause you’ll give me long answer. How did they manage?”

“In 1945, when Anglo-American and Soviet troops entered the concentration camps, they discovered piles of corpses, bones, and human ashes—testimony to Nazi mass murder. Soldiers also found thousands of Jewish and non-Jewish survivors suffering from starvation and disease. For these survivors, especially Jewish survivors, life was very difficult for several years."

"How did little Marianne make it?"

"Randy, the devastation that followed the war included the broken marriage of Marianne's parents, Tilly and Jakob. Neither one was able to mend the other's broken heart, nor care for their only child. Their no-fault divorce with joint custody of Marianne, who had been taken to live with her grandparents, became final in 1947. The best efforts of the Marshall Plan were unable to reunite Marianne's family. I'll tell you more if you want, Randy. Next time I'll tell you about how the war affected the United States."

"You've got me hooked now, Joe, but first tell me about Marianne."

Marianne

1945-1950

After all her terrible experiences of air-raids, illnesses, cold and hunger, Marianne found a new world in Macken which seemed like heaven on Earth to her. Emaciated and suffering from an eye infection, she and her mother arrived at her grandparents' home after another harrowing train ride followed by a bumpy ride in a wagon drawn by cows.

The house in the Hunsrück Mountains was the very one in which Oma, Marianne's grandmother Maria, was born. The house, and in fact the entire village of Macken, had remained essentially the same since Maria had left it as a fourteen-year-old girl in 1902.

It was a two-story homestead built in the nineteenth century, but it had remained intact despite the two world wars. Maria's older sister Katherine was still living there with her husband Nikola. Part of the ground floor, which had been a small "Gasthaus" (restaurant) in better times, was rented to strangers, but the kitchen and the upstairs rooms were still available for the family. There was no indoor plumbing except for one seldom-functioning sink in the common downstairs kitchen. Primitive electric wiring had been installed, but electricity only flowed sporadically during the post-war years. Tilly, who had enjoyed city life before the war hated this place, especially because of the outdoor privy. She planned to leave as soon as possible. The warmth of loving arms and appetizing food, however, won Marianne's heart forever.

Oma and Opa, as she called her grandparents, had somehow transformed the upstairs rooms into a clean, cheerful apartment. When they fled Koblenz, they had brought some furniture with them.

"Oma, that's the same beautiful stove you had in Koblenz." Marianne was nosing all around the kitchen despite her sore eyes.

"Yes, it was difficult to get it up here to Macken, but a friend with a truck helped me move my pride and joy."

"Oma, what are these little handles?"

"Those are to use with natural gas, but I'll have to cook with wood or coal here in Macken. We don't have gas pipes in this house. See, the wood or a coal briquette goes into this fire box. When the wood burns, the top will heat up and cook whatever is in the pots."

"Will we have lots of food? I was often very hungry in St. Wolfgang. Sometimes we only got some soup I didn't like."

"Child, did you get a look at the garden yet? Opa and I are growing vegetables. Opa will also help the farmers with their work in exchange for food. I promise, we won't starve if I have anything to say about it."

Even while the bombing in Koblenz sent people to the bomb shelters Marianne's grandmother had often expressed her opinion about the necessity of food.

The stove was a white enamel monster with shiny chrome legs a handrail and handles, a well-scrubbed cooking surface, and a black pipe which conducted the smoke up a chimney. Smoke? Yes. It was a modern coal-or-wood burner which had a side panel with knobs for natural gas. There were no gas pipes in the village, so Oma had to fire up the stove with wood before she could do any cooking.

A few other familiar things had also been carted to Macken. The kitchen was furnished with the table and chairs that matched the precious "Schrank." (A schrank is a free-standing kitchen cupboard with decorative glass panels in the doors.) Marianne recognized many items which had been rescued from the city apartment that Oma and Opa had been forced to abandon. A couch, some books, a bed, a large framed picture, a few tools, some kitchen utensils, some clothes and linens all had been trucked to Macken by a friend. This friend was allowed to keep his truck for private business because he had also done some trucking for local Nazi officials during the war. Moving furniture was very complicated. No one had private transportation without special permission. There were no cars, and people had to travel by trains which were crowded and slow.

Marianne was happily touching all the familiar things, but when she overheard her mother telling Oma that she was leaving, tears started to roll down her cheeks.

"Marianne, don't cry. I'll come back to visit whenever I can. I have to go back to Koblenz."

"Why?"

"In Koblenz I'll be able to earn a living. People will need clothes, and I know how to sew and repair clothes. I can't stay here in Macken because there is not enough work for me."

Tilly knew that her little daughter would be well taken care of. Most importantly, there would be enough food in this country village where the people lived off the land.

Macken, a village of about eighty small family farms with about four hundred residents, only had two streets laid out in a T-shape. The steep road approaching Macken passed the town's cemetery. There were eight small farms on that road before it ended at the street that ran smack through the middle of the village. This main street branched off to the left and the right with approximately half of the eighty farm houses in the "Unterdorf" (the lower village) and half in the "Oberdorf" (the upper village). Separating them was the village square where the villagers met on Sundays after church. The church with its rectory was adjacent to the square, and on the other side stood the community "Backes" (the bake house, an open shed with two giant wood-fired brick ovens where the villagers took turns baking their bread). This area was the hub of town activities.

"Oma, why does it always smell so good around the Backes?"

"Marianne, that's where people bake their bread. What you smell is fresh bread being pulled out of the oven."

"Can I watch?"

“Yes, next week, I’ll be taking another turn to bake bread. You can help me and watch the whole thing. You already had a piece of the bread I baked yesterday. How did you like it?”

“It was yummy with the raspberry jam, Oma.”

Since there were only two large ovens in the community Backes, there had to be a fair system of time-sharing that allowed everyone to get their baking done. A tradition of drawing lots had evolved over the years that served the purpose of choosing who went first, second, and so on the next morning.

Every morning at ten o’clock, those women who wished to use the oven on the following day would gather in front of the Backes. Each would bring a twig and a sharp knife. While chatting, they would then cut an inch-long piece off the twig and carve a special design into the bark. When everyone was satisfied with her token, it was tossed into the upturned apron of one of the women. One of the children watching the ritual then reached into the apron and drew the lots out, one at a time. The order of the draw determined the order of the starting times of the following day's baking.

After chatting for a few more minutes, the women went home to prepare the dough. In a wooden trough, specially reserved for bread-making, a large amount of flour was heaped high and shaped into a crater. A sourdough leavening saved from the previous week's baking would be mixed with liquid and poured into the hollowed-out spot. Some of the flour was mixed with it and then left to rise. Later, the kneading would begin. The dough had to be kneaded several times and left to rise. That evening, the house always smelled promising. By the next day, the dough would be ready to be shaped into loaves.

The dough, along with enough wood to bake it, was taken in bulk to the Backes. Anywhere from six to ten loaves would be shaped out of the amorphous mass on a sparkling clean butcher block table and baked at once in the fired up oven. Large wooden scrapers were used to remove the cinders, and then wooden paddles were used to push the loaves far back into the hot chamber. Sometimes there would be a little lump of dough left over; not enough for another loaf of bread but just enough for an apple cake!

"Marianne, today we'll bake bread. And a surprise for you."

"What is it, Oma?"

"Not so nosy, young lady. You'll see. Go grab a couple of apples, and come with me."

At the Backes, Oma worked hard to get everything done within her time slot. Once the bread was safely baking in the fire chamber, she peeled and diced the apples and kneaded them into the bit of left-over dough. "Now all it needs is a little bit of sugar, but I forgot to bring it."

"Oma, I can run home and get some. I'll be right back. I know what you're making. Is that the special surprise you promised?"

"Yes, let's call it an Apfelplatz (Apple cookie). My mother used to bake these for me when I was a little girl like you."

Marianne happily ran home for the sugar. Her war-torn little soul was beginning to heal. Oma had used an old remedy to save her eyes. For ten minutes twice a day, with a towel draped over her head, Marianne had to lean over a steaming bowl of chamomile tea. "See? All the coal dust from the train ride is being pulled out by the chamomile tea. Pretty soon, your eyes will be nice and clear again,"

Oma had promised. Now Marianne was running around like any other healthy child in the village.

"Here's the sugar, Oma."

Two other important public buildings completed the village: the school and the forest ranger's residence overlooking the upper end of the town. Two tiny general stores where one could purchase such items as sugar or shoelaces, a shoe repair shop, a smithy, one public telephone at the makeshift Post Office, a shepherd and a few other services were scattered throughout the town and privately maintained.

* * *

"Marianne, today we're going to harvest peas on our leased field," announced Oma one morning.

"What is a leased field, Oma?" interrupted Marianne.

"Most of the farmers own their fields, but we don't own any. The fields are usually inherited from one generation to another. Our family doesn't own any fields anymore. So every year we lease, that is like rent, a few of the fields that belong to the parish. We also rent a large walnut tree and four apple trees. We have to pay rent to the parish every year. Whatever we plant and harvest, we get to keep without having to buy it in a store. We have one field with peas and one with Kabbes..."

Marianne interrupted her again, "Oma, what is Kabbes?"

"Oh, I forgot to tell you. Kabbes is what is called cabbage in city language. Out of Kabbes we can make sauerkraut. Now let me finish my story about leased fields. We also have two fields for potatoes and one field for turnips. Remember? You like the Rübenkraut (thick dark syrup) I make out of the sugar beets."

"Yummy, Rübenkraut is especially good on buttered bread, but it is always so sticky," Marianne laughed. "I always have to wash my hands after I eat Rübenkraut."

"You should wash your hands before eating, too! You're sweet, but you won't melt with a little bit of water," teased Oma. "Now we're going to make our sandwiches to take with us, and we'll also take a bottle of raspberry juice. We have a lot of work to do today and probably won't get home till this evening."

Working in the fields was always a treat for the village children, no matter whether the adults were picking peas, cutting hay, or harvesting wheat. The grain harvest was especially exciting. After a farmer cut the stalks with a scythe, his wife bound them into bundles which were then stacked for drying. The children ran around the stacks to play hide and seek. A few days later the dried stacks were carted back to the farm on wagons pulled by cows. Sometimes a farmer let a couple of children ride home on a wagon piled high with wheat or rye.

One time the wagon happened to hit a rut in the unpaved primitive road, "I'm scared! Let me off," yelled Marianne. The whole wagon was shaking and swaying precariously from side to side, threatening her with injury.

"Just hold on to the ropes, Marianne." The ropes were holding the bales together. "Nothing bad is going to happen."

Fear mixed with excitement until the slow-moving procession and sweaty faces finally reached the village. With a sigh of relief, Marianne and the other children jumped off and scampered home.

* * *

After dinner Marianne was usually allowed to go play outside until it got dark. Throughout the village the farmers were hammering their scythes to sharpen them for the next day's cutting. Mixed with the rhythmic hammering, the chickens cackling, cows mooing and children screaming at play, the village evenings rang out with peace and joy. Sometimes Opa opened a window and played his concertina to entertain the whole street of people. Strains of familiar folksongs told everyone that all was well with the world again. Nothing could match the peaceful summer evenings in Macken.

Because Opa had been a railroad engineer before he retired, he still owned a few tools. He had become the handyman on whom everyone in the village depended. He repaired broken things, soldered metal containers and sharpened knives and scissors on the grindstone that had been in the backyard of the old homestead for longer than anyone could remember.

Opa always treated Marianne with love and tenderness. He taught her how to play cards and told her tall tales about his experiences as a soldier in World War I. He taught her how to sing songs, and accompanied her on his concertina.

* * *

"Opa, why is your workshop way up in the loft? Do I have to use this ladder to get up there?"

"Well, there are no stairs, so I made this sturdy wooden ladder. Come, I'll climb up first and then you can climb up. When you get to the top, I'll help you step into my workshop."

Nervously, but brave and very curious, Marianne climbed up. She inspected the entire loft. "Oh, Opa, there are rabbits in that cage! I love rabbits."

“Alright, you get to come up here and feed the rabbits every day from now on. You can pet them, but if you let them out, they might run away and hide, so be careful!”

“What do they eat?”

“They like carrots. Oma will let you take the green tops off the carrots. Sometimes you can give them a whole carrot or some other leaves.”

* * *

The farms were tiny self-sustaining estates consisting of a residence, a barn, a stall for the livestock, a yard for the chickens and a small garden for growing vegetables. Some had a few fruit trees growing in a backyard. Only three buildings in this town had indoor plumbing: the rectory, the school and the forest ranger’s home. All the farms had outhouses next to a manure pile.

“Oma, Bah! that manure stinks! Why do they have to pile it up in the yard?”

“The farmers use the manure to make plants grow. It’s all part of nature.”

“But why does it stink like that?”

“Because of the cow dung. In the mornings, the farmers use their pitchforks to remove the dirty straw from the stalls and toss it on top of the manure pile. Then they put fresh straw under the cows.”

“Oh, I watched our neighbor do that, but I didn’t know what it was for.”

"It's very important to clean the stalls every day, so the cows won't get sick. The clean straw gets soaked and dirty during the day, and the next morning the farmer has to remove it."

Those manure piles were carefully tended at each farm because they were used as compost during the planting season. Most of the homes were two-story houses with no running water. Each yard had its own brick-lined well with a bucket on a rope suspended from a hand-cranked pulley. The water in the wells came from the water table deep in the Earth. There was, of course, no way to keep the seepage from the manure piles completely out of the water source, so all water for human consumption had to be boiled. This contamination was one of the reasons that Tilly hated Macken. On the other hand, as a child, Marianne was oblivious to such matters. To her, the entire village with its bomb-free sky was simply Mother Nature.

* * *

Soon after her arrival, Marianne's health improved. There was talk of school, and she could hardly wait. School would start as soon as a teacher was found. Finally, an elderly man was hired by the mayor of the town. He didn't last long. As a former music teacher, weary from the war and its aftermath, all he tried to teach was some music. The children were hungry for REAL learning, like math and language. They didn't just want to sing for this man. Discipline became impossible, and soon that teacher was sent packing. Good teachers were difficult to find, however. The children had to wait some more. The Priest, Herr Otto Andreas, tried to fill in with weekly Catechism lessons, but the children were getting very impatient and out of control. The whole town was excited when Herr Zensen, an educated man, moved into the school's upstairs apartment with his wife. His wife, Frau Zensen, was very ill, so she seldom came out of the apartment, but Herr Zensen proved to be the excellent teacher the children of Macken needed.

There were around sixty students ages six through fourteen. Herr Zensen kept all of them under control in one large classroom. Sometimes he let one or two of the older students work with the little ones. He never lost his temper, but he was a strong disciplinarian. At first the children behaved because they were grateful to have a good teacher. Later they behaved well because he had gently taught them exactly how respectfully he expected children to act. Two times a week, Herr Andreas, the Priest, came to school to teach Catechism. On Saturday mornings, a woman from another village came to teach the girls handicrafts while Herr Zensen took the boys to the school garden to teach them gardening skills. Marianne took to this routine like a duck takes to water. She had found her comfort zone at last!

She even found friends! There was one family that had six children. Marianne loved visiting them because they treated her as a sister. The oldest, Martha, was two years ahead of Marianne in school, but she was the one who became her best friend. They spent hours reading or doing needlework. Marianne had a secret crush on her younger brother Gerhard.

She also befriended the children of a couple of other families. Hiltrud who was a little younger than Marianne lived next door. The two girls invented a game that kept them amused for hours and hours. They called this game "Hannele" (short for handeln, = to trade). Each girl kept a folder with all kinds of paper scraps, such as stickers, old bills, pictures, and anything that had some print on it. They spread their folders on a table and started trading. There were no fancy trading cards, but they took their trading game just as seriously as traders of any generation.

Electric service was sporadic, so no one depended on the radio or lights. There were so many wonderful things to keep the children entertained in village life that no one was ever bored. the children amused themselves with the natural resources on the land. Climbing trees, especially during the time when fresh ripe fruit could be eaten directly off the branches was a favorite pastime. There were plenty of nooks and crannies for playing "hide and seek." The dusk hour was a favorite time to run around and play "catch" or "hide and seek." After dark, people remained indoors and used homemade candles to light their way around the house.

Another exciting pastime for the children was watching the annual slaughters throughout the village in October and November. One of the farmers in Macken was also a trained butcher. He had the skills and equipment to provide slaughtering services to all the other farmers. Each family needed to slaughter at least one large pig to provide the Speck (smoked bacon), Schinken (ham) and Wurst (sausages) for the rest of the year.

One slaughter started early in the morning and took nearly all day. The pig had to be "bled" by hanging it up for several hours. Certain parts, such as the feet, had to be submersed in a tub of boiling water for sanitary handling. Some of the meat was salted, smoked or canned. Sausages which would keep for several weeks were cooked and preserved. All of this took place in the front yard in full view of anyone. Groups of children gathered around each slaughter to watch. Now and then a naughty boy might pick up a discarded tail and run away.

One time a boy wrapped up a tail in some paper. He planned to present it to Marianne's old aunt, Tante Katt. Marianne watched him pretend that it was a sausage sent as a present from a neighbor. Tante Katt discovered the trick immediately and took off after him with a broom. He was too fast for her and got away. Tante Katt just stood there still waving the broomstick in the air. Oma caught Marianne laughing at the whole scene.

"Marianne, come here. I'm disappointed in you. Tante Katt is my sister, and I expect you to respect her."

"But Oma, you should have seen her face. I had to laugh when she grabbed that broom and tried to catch that boy."

"Enough! Tonight you get no dessert, and I expect you to apologize to Tante Katt. Why don't you make her a pretty bouquet for her table? You can use one of our vases."

Marianne quickly ran off to gather some wildflowers. Tante Katt gratefully gave her a big hug and all was forgotten.

A group of Marianne's friends especially enjoyed playing in the woods behind the schoolhouse. There was a fire look-out with a platform. The children climbed up the rickety ladder and played "house" on the platform for hours. They had gathered a variety of shards and other rubble as furnishings. They pretended to be families living a normal life visiting each other. When they got tired of playing house, they went on outings in the Wäldche.

The "Wäldche" was a small forest of about a square mile. On one side it was bordered by the main road leading to the neighboring village. There were no wild animals or poisonous plants. In the fall, the children picked blueberries right off the mossy forest floor. They were also intrigued by a small brick building close to the road. It was apparently the town's water pump which did not work regularly because of the sporadic electricity.

It was a special treat to climb on top of the building and yell down a large vent pipe. Strange echoes from within the building added to their delight as they told each other scary stories.

Several other forests, which were not so child-friendly, offered resources, such as hazelnuts, mushrooms, beechnuts or acorns to the villagers. In late fall, many groups of adults went into the woods to harvest the bounty of nature, especially the beechnuts. Opa had fashioned a large sieve to separate the leaves, twigs and other debris from the actual nuts. The nuts were then put into large burlap sacks and carted home.

At home Oma and Marianne spent the evenings sorting them. No outer shells, pebbles or twigs! When several bags of the well-sorted triangular beech-nuts had been gathered, it was time for a visit to the "Ölmühle" (oil mill).

"Oma! That was hard work. Look at my fingers. The sharp corners cut them."

"Here, let's wash your hands. The beechnuts have to be out of the outer shell, or the Ölmühle won't accept them. It's alright to leave the actual nut in the husk though. We will get a liter of oil for every "Zentner" (100 kilograms) of beechnuts."

Marianne was impressed by the big machines in the Ölmühle. Fascinated she watched the water wheel behind the building. As the wheel turned it set the noisy machines inside the building into motion. The loud rumbling and heat kept Marianne at a safe distance while the miller and his helper operated the mill.

Marianne caught the miller's eye. "I know that we're going to get a bottle of cooking oil, but what are you going to do with all the rest of the stuff?"

"We get to keep the remainder of oil as well as the husks. See, this machine makes bricks out of the husks. We then sell these as fuel for the winter. It's a trade."

Marianne smiled, “Oh, I know about trading. My friend and I trade stickers and other stuff.”

The miller smiled back. No money was needed for this deal. People gathered the beechnuts, and his oil mill had the necessary machines. The machines ran on energy produced on the premises by a giant waterwheel in the creek behind the building. This barter system was satisfactory for everyone involved.

There were other mills in the area.

One mill was in a village about two miles north of Macken. “Come with us, Marianne. Opa and I are taking this rye to Dommershausen.”

“What?”

“We will need enough flour for bread to get us through the winter.”

“Can I use the scooter Mutti brought me last time she visited?”

“Yes, that a good idea. It’s only about two miles away. I’ll pull the cart, and you can ride your scooter,” Opa agreed.

The mill in Dommershausen is where the farmers took the grain, usually rye, to be milled into flour. The miller kept some of the flour as payment for his work. This mill was very primitive. Giant stone wheels ground the grain. Another more modern mill was located about five miles south of Macken. That’s where the farmers took the wheat to be milled into the finer cake flour.

The villages in these mountains were truly self-sufficient and self-sustaining.

The annually-grown produce included potatoes, cabbage, turnips, beans, peas, apples, and beets. Nearly every home had a garden for fresh green vegetables throughout the summer and fall. All the farmers preserved whatever wasn't eaten. The potatoes were kept in the cool root-cellars under the homes. The cabbages were pickled into sauerkraut which was kept in large stone crocks. Beans and peas were dried and kept in bags in the home. Fresh string beans were thinly sliced and pickled. Beets were pickled. Those turnips which were to be used as vegetables through the winter were kept in dug-out trenches in the backyards, while the sugar beet turnips were boiled down into Rübenkraut, a thick syrup which could be used as a spread on bread or as a sweetener for baked goods. Apples were cut up and dried on strings. Other fruit and berries were canned or preserved in jams, jellies or juice concentrates.

"Oma, you have a lot of work to do all the time," Marianne was amazed at her grandmother's strength and energy.

"Child, I've been working since I was your age. I learned how to do all this farm work while I was growing up right here in this same house."

"I like watching you, Oma. I'm going to be a grandmother someday and take good care of my grandchildren like you do."

"That's a good plan, Marianne, and I hope you have a good husband to help you."

"Like Opa?"

"Yes, like Opa."

Opa especially prized the overripe fruit that had fallen on the ground under the trees. Large crocks of rotting apples, pears, plums and cherries fermented in a shed next to the manure pile every summer. Marianne's curiosity grew as she wondered whether she would have to eat the smelly stuff brewing in those earthenware crocks. Eventually, she found out what was happening: Opa was preparing the ingredients for Moonshine!

Whenever Opa decided that the fruit had fermented enough (usually once a month), he brought a large kettle with copper tubing into Oma's precious kitchen, and the party and the fighting would begin. Opa and a couple of his card-playing friends distilled the fermented brew into a very potent schnapps.

"What is that, Opa?" Marianne asked as she watched the clear liquid drip from the tubing.

Opa laughed, "Here, hold your finger under the end of the tube." Marianne felt a warm drop of liquid on the tip of her finger. "Now taste it."

"Aaaah!" she yelled. The stuff was so strong, Marianne could barely breathe. "Ouch!" Opa and his friends, laughed. Oma yelled at them.

"Leave that child alone. That stuff is not good for her, and you shouldn't be drinking it either!" But the guys loved sipping on this brew. Naturally, they always became quite intoxicated by the end of the day. There was always a battle when Opa got drunk. Oma and Marianne sometimes went to sleep at her friend's house when Opa got too wild and snored loudly in his drunken sleep.

Opa was a lamb when he was sober. He spent hours in his make-shift workshop repairing broken farm equipment and creating useful items out of stuff he found around the village. There was always plenty of food because the farmers gave him food in exchange for his services. He loved making toys for Marianne and her friends. One day he came up with a wood and wire design for little doll chairs of every size. Nearly every child in the village had stilts made by him. The boys especially liked the trains he made from simple leftover pieces of wood. They even had metal-trimmed wheels!

Opa's resourcefulness included musical talent. He owned a small "Ziehharmonika" which is a type of accordion (or concertina) with buttons for both hands. Whenever the weather was balmy, he sat near an open window after the evening meal and played folk songs for the neighborhood.

* * *

Macken was a magic place in winter. Shiny icicles draped from the eaves. Trees and bushes were covered with snow, and windows were frosted in intricate patterns. Snow and ice often covered the street in the Oberdorf (upper village). The children rode their wooden sleds right down the middle of the road. It was difficult to stay warm enough, but the homemade sweaters and mittens helped a lot. Oma spent a lot of time knitting. Marianne loved most of the things she made, but she couldn't stand one sweater she knitted with wool from a local sheep.

"Bah, Oma. This sweater stinks like a manure pile."

"I noticed that while I was knitting it. I suspect that my friend Lucia didn't wash all the dinkleberries out of the raw fleece before she it spun into the yarn. I'll wash the sweater a couple of times and let the sun bleach all the dinkleberries out."

Marianne liked the word "dinkleberries." "What are dinkleberries, Oma?"

"Dried poop from the sheep," laughed Oma.

Marianne enjoyed watching the whole process of getting the wool from the sheep to actually wearing the nice clean sweater.

Every fall the town shepherd sold fleece of raw wool directly off the shorn sheep. First the hanks had to be washed and bleached. Once the fleece of wool was dry it could be spun. Almost all the elderly women in town owned spinning wheels. In the evenings, after the day's work was done, they loved sitting around, spinning the wool into thin strands of yarn while making small-talk. Sometimes I got to help wind the yarn into balls. Often the pungent natural smell of the sheep's wool was not washed out adequately. Consequently, the garments knitted from this wool had the same pungent aroma.

The social life of the people depended on the seasonal changes. In the spring, the fields had to be plowed and sowed. Gardens were replanted, and calves, lambs, piglets, chicks and other animals were born. In the summer the farm work didn't stop till sundown. Stalls had to be kept clean, cows had to be milked, tools repaired and sharpened, fields worked and the winter food supply preserved. In the fall, the harvest and the butchering began in earnest. In the winter, man and nature rested.

In Macken young Marianne became strong and healthy. She found the healing quietude of nature and learned to live in harmony with the seasons of the land and animals.

* * *

Strangely, one of the most pleasant places Marianne discovered in Macken was a cemetery. A cemetery pleasant? Yes. Just outside the village, this very special fenced-in garden welcomed her whenever she wanted to be truly safe and alone. The villagers customarily planted lots of flowers on all the graves. There was a special area for children who had died before they turned six. Their headstones were decorated with tiny angel statues of white marble. The inscriptions on the all the graves simply declared the existence of a named person from one date to another. Marianne walked among the graves, reading the names and dates and thinking of the people under the ground. At other times she thought long and hard about Jesus in the Garden of Gethsemane, trying to imagine what it must have been like for Him. She often stopped to pray by the particularly large headstone of a village priest from long ago.

Sometimes Marianne invited a couple of friends, “Let’s go sing for the “souls” in the cemetery.” The small group of children then sang and walked around happily, but they never disrespected the spirit of the place. Sometimes they talked about the things that might have killed the people buried there. It never occurred to Marianne to be afraid. It was simply a place of eternal peace.

The unconditional love of her grandparents, the resourceful farmers, the mischievous children, the seasonal changes of the land and its rich harvests have given her a lasting respect for life on Earth. In 1945 Marianne arrived as a broken little girl. By 1950 she was ready to take on the challenges of a future in a completely different world.

In the Museum

"So Randy, what do you know about the Aftermath of World War II in the United States?"

They had decided to go back to the museum where they first met a few months before.

Randy looked sheepish, "To tell you the truth, we haven't been studying about World War Two in history class anymore, so I kinda lost interest."

"But you called me. Why?"

"I missed our talks. Besides, I'd really like to find out more about these two kids."

Joe said, “Before I can tell you about Leighton, I’m going to explain how World War II affected life in the United States.”

“Works for me, Joe.”

“While daily life went on for most American families after the war, the negative effects of World War II were felt primarily among the Gold Star families who had suffered the very personal loss of a husband, son or daughter and the Japanese families who had been interned in various camps.”

“Gold Star families, Joe?”

“On May 28, 1918, President Wilson approved a suggestion made by the Women's Committee of the Council of National Defenses that, instead of wearing conventional mourning for relatives who have died in the service of their country, American women should wear a black band on the left arm with a gilt star on the band for each member of the family who has given his life for the nation.

The term Gold Star Mothers, as applied to mothers whose sons or daughters died in World War I, was accepted and continued to be used in reference to all American military engagements since that time.”

“Oh,” nodded Randy.

“The lives of most Americans were positively affected by World War II. Returning servicemen and women were welcomed back into society. The Servicemen's Readjustment Act of 1944 (P.L. 78-346) was enacted.

Known informally as the G.I. Bill, this law provided a range of benefits for returning World War II veterans (commonly referred to as G.I.s-Government Issues)."

Randy smiled, "I remember you called yourself G.I. Joe when we first met. Is that what you were referring to?"

"Yes, I took advantage of the benefits which included low-cost mortgages, low-interest loans to start a business, cash payments of tuition and living expenses to attend university, high school or vocational education, as well as one year of unemployment compensation. It was available to every veteran who had been on active duty during the war years for at least one-hundred twenty days and had not been dishonorably discharged; combat was not required. By 1956, roughly 2.2 million veterans had used the G.I. Bill education benefits in order to attend colleges or universities, and an additional 5.6 million used these benefits for some kind of training program.

Historians and economists judge the G.I. Bill a major political and economic success—especially in contrast to the treatments of World War I veterans—and a major contribution to America's stock of human capital that sped long-term economic growth."

"That's cool. You mentioned something about the Japanese, but I forgot what it was."

"Japanese-American life changed again after World War Two."

"How so?"

"After World War II in the year 1948, President Truman signed the Japanese-American Claims Act. This act was a way to compensate Japanese Americans for their economic losses due to their forced evacuation. Although some $38 million was to be paid out through provisions of the act, it would be largely ineffective even on the limited scope in which it operated."

Randy interrupted him, "Joe, did Mr. Matsuyama get some of that money?"

"Probably. He had enough money to buy his store back, remember?" Joe reminded Randy. "Officially, the policy toward Japanese also changed after the war."

"How's that?"

"With the McCarran-Walter Act: When the war ended, the American opinion of Japanese was changed. Japan was in the process of rebuilding with the help of the U.S. military. Japanese became known for their intelligence, amiable relations, and hardworking ethic. The new perspective of this country changed American minds about Japanese. In 1952, this new opinion of the Japanese resulted in first-generation Japanese Americans receiving the right to become naturalized U.S. citizens with the McCarran-Walter Act."

"That's good. I have a lot of Japanese and part Japanese friends in High School."

Joe agreed, "Yes, times are different now."

Randy wondered, "But Leighton's family was Chinese. How were they affected?"

"Oh, there was also an important effect on Chinese-Americans as a result of the war. The Magnuson Act, also known as the Chinese Exclusion Repeal Act of 1943, was immigration legislation proposed by U.S. Representative (later Senator) Warren G. Magnuson of Washington and signed into law on December 17, 1943, in the United States. It allowed Chinese immigration for the first time since the Chinese Exclusion Act of 1882, and permitted Chinese nationals already residing in the country to become naturalized citizens. This marked the first time since the Naturalization Act of 1790 that any Asians were permitted to be naturalized."

"Did that affect Leighton's family?"

"Not right away, but as the boys grew up, they became more and more American. It was a very slow process."

"Oh. I guess new laws take a long time to affect families."

"That's right. Only since the 1940s when the United States and China became allies during World War II, did the situation for Chinese Americans begin to improve, as restrictions on entry into the country, naturalization and mixed marriage were being lessened. In 1943, Chinese immigration to the United States was once again permitted—by way of the Magnuson Act—thereby repealing 61 years of official racial discrimination against the Chinese. Large-scale Chinese immigration did not occur until 1965 when the Immigration and Nationality Act of 1965 lifted national origin quotas. After World War II, anti-Asian prejudice began to decrease, and Chinese immigrants, along with other Asians (such as Japanese, Koreans, Indians and Vietnamese), have adapted and advanced. Currently, the Chinese constitute the largest ethnic group of Asian Americans (about 22%), and have confounded earlier expectations that they would form an indigestible mass in American society. For example, many Chinese Americans of American birth may know little or nothing about traditional Chinese culture, just as European Americans and African Americans may know little or nothing about the original cultures of their ancestors."

"Is that what happened to Leighton? Does he know about the culture of his ancestors?"

"Well, Randy, Leighton grew up in Los Angeles. You can imagine how that big city with all the different people who live there influenced his life. There is one important factor we haven't even talked about yet."

"Oh? What's that?"

"Miscegenation."

"Huh? Miscegenation?"

Joe explained, “In the United States, various anti-miscegenation State laws prohibited marriages between whites and blacks, and in many States they also prohibited marriages between whites and Native Americans or Asians. In the U.S., such laws were known as anti-miscegenation laws. From 1913 until 1948, 30 out of the then 48 states enforced such laws. Although an "Anti-Miscegenation Amendment" to the United States Constitution was proposed in 1871, in 1912–1913, and again in 1928, no nationwide law against racially mixed marriages was ever enacted. In 1967, the United States Supreme Court unanimously ruled in *Loving v. Virginia* that anti-miscegenation laws are unconstitutional. With this ruling, these anti-miscegenation laws were no longer in effect in the remaining 16 states that still had them.”

“Dang! I never heard of that. No wonder there’s so much trouble between the races.”

“Yes, the laws were strict in some places and not so strict in others. That makes for a lot of confusion and prejudice especially for people who fall in love.”

Randy’s eyes lit up. “I bet Leighton and Marianne had a lot of trouble getting together.”

“Hold on. You’re getting way ahead of the story. I’m not going to tell you about how they got together until after I explain a few more things about the effect of the Aftermath on Leighton.”

“Okay, okay, I’ll be patient.”

“Actually, there was no immediate effect on Leighton, Jack sold the grocery store back to the former owner, and Jack’s family benefitted in various ways from the easing of tensions between Asian immigrants and native-born Americans. It’s also important to the story that you know a bit more about the aftermath of World War II in the whole world.”

“Oh, the whole world? Is that why it was called a world war?”

“Right. The world leaders realized that something had to be done.”

Randy scratched his head, “Man with so much trouble and hate and prejudice, how can anyone do anything to stop wars?”

“Well, some world leaders tried when they established the United Nations. The UN is an intergovernmental organization to promote international co-operation. As part of the aftermath of World War Two, the UN was established on 24 October 1945 in order to prevent another such conflict. At its founding, the UN had 51 member states; there are now 193. The headquarters of the United Nations is in Manhattan, New York City, Further main offices are situated in Geneva, Nairobi and Vienna. The organization is financed by assessed and voluntary contributions from its member states. Its objectives include maintaining international peace and security, promoting human rights, fostering social and economic development, protecting the environment, and providing humanitarian aid in cases of famine, natural disaster, and armed conflict.”

"That sounds great! Did the United Nations keep the world safe for Leighton and Marianne while they were growing up?" wondered Randy.

"Well, listen and I'll tell you."

Leighton

1945-47

"Hey Dad, Did you hear that the war is over?"

"Yes, it was in the newspapers," answered Jack, but he wasn't convinced. "*There's always going to be some kind of war in the world,*" he thought.

"Is Auntie Number Three going to bring Emily back from China now?"

"I don't think Emily will ever come back to America."

"What? Why not? She's my sister. Why can't she live with us?"

"I got a letter not too long ago from Auntie Number Seven. She said that Auntie Number Three had died, so Emily is living with her now."

"With Auntie Number Seven?"

"Yes."

"So is Auntie Number Seven bringing Emily back?"

"No."

"Dad…."

"Look, Lai, I don't really want to talk about this. Let Emily grow up in China with her cousins. She's going to school. She's happy there."

"But, but…"

"No more discussion," Jack walked away.

* * *

"Hey Dad, the mailman just came by. Here's a letter from Mr. Matsuyama," Leighton was just arriving at his dad's store, so he brought in the mail.

"Let me see, Lai." Jack had heard that Manzanar was closing now that the war was over. "I wonder why he's writing me."

Leighton suggested, "Maybe he wants to buy his store back."

"That would be alright with me. It's a lot of work to own and run a store. Allen is busy with his tennis and hardly ever comes in to help."

"Well, Dad, what does the letter say?"

"You were right, Lai. Mr. Matsuyama and his family are coming back to Los Angeles. He says how much he misses his store.

I'll offer him his store back. This would mean that we could move closer to Chinatown. I should be able to get a job in one of the stores there."

"When is he coming back?"

"He'll arrive next week. The government is trying to get all the Japanese moved out of Manzanar as soon as possible."

"I'm sure you and Mr. Matsuyama will work it out. I remember when you got money from the bank to buy the store. Is Mr. Matsuyama going to borrow money from the bank too?"

"Probably. He might even have some money left from when he sold me the store. Now let's get some of these supplies on the shelves. Customers will be coming in to buy groceries for dinner."

The following week Mr. Matsuyama walked into the store. "Hello Jack. I see that you took good care of business. You makin' a profit?"

"Well, it's picked up since the end of the war. For a couple of years, it was a bit slow, but now people are feeling good about the economy again. What about you and your family?"

Mr. Matsuyama frowned a little, "We had a pretty hard time at Manzanar, but the family stayed healthy, and I think I'd like to open a grocery store again."

Jack wondered whether he should offer to sell him the store back, "Are you staying in Los Angeles?"

"Yes, I've lived in this city since my parents brought me here. My wife was born here, and our three children have gone to school here. This city is my home. I've been wondering whether you'd be interested in selling me the store back."

Jack took a deep breath. He was relieved that he didn't have to bring up the subject. "I suppose we could make a deal that would benefit both of us," he smiled.

"Let's go to the same bank where we did business before."

"How about tomorrow morning around ten. I'll meet you there," offered Jack.

* * *

Jack proudly told his boys that he had made a good deal with Mr. Matsuyama. "Now I have some money for a down payment on a house. The credit manager at the bank said that my credit was good."

"Leighton wondered, "Credit? What's that?"

"Well, it means faith. The people who put money into the bank believe that the bank will keep it safe. The bankers who let people borrow money believe that the people will pay it back. When I owned the store, I was very good about paying back money every month, so they believe that I'll be reliable in the future. That means I have credit."

"Oh, that makes sense. Are you going to borrow money from the bank to buy a house?"

"Yes, I have some money saved up, and I'll borrow the rest."

Leighton was a little nervous about moving again. He was in the seventh grade at Virgil Junior High and just getting used to making new friends. *"I wonder where Dad is going to find a house for us."*

After only six months at Virgil, Leighton started at Nightingale Junior High. Jack had found an affordable house on Cleveland Street.

“Man! This house is a wreck. It needs a lot of work.” Allen grumbled something about spending more time at Echo Park instead of this “ugly” place. “Are you going to bring Mom home now?”

“No.” Jack knew it was not a very good house, but it was what he could afford. “Mom is still sick. I can’t take care of her.”

* * *

The boys had become quite resourceful at making money for their own expenses. Leighton’s shoe shine business and newspaper route were keeping him quite busy. Allen obtained his tennis equipment for helping the director at Echo Park, and he also had a newspaper route to earn pocket money.

“Allen, did you hear that Mom’s brothers are getting out of the army?”

“No, how do you know?”

“When I went with Dad to visit Mom last Sunday, they were talking about it. Both Harry and George got drafted and had to serve in the war. Now they’re getting an honorable discharge.”

“I wonder what that is.”

Leighton speculated, “I think it’s like a report card in school. If you do your work and don’t screw up, you get good grades. If you do a good job in the army you get an honorable discharge when you get out.”

“That makes sense,” Allen agreed. “You want to go play some tennis later?”

“No, I’m meeting some guys at the bowling lanes. There’s some pretty cool guys at Nightingale.”

A group of seventh, eighth and ninth graders from Nightingale often met at Angeles Bowling Lanes after school.

Besides the bowling lanes, there were pool and billiard tables to keep the boys occupied. Despite being one of the youngest, Leighton excelled at bowling and billiards and often won money off the older boys.

Frank, a ninth grader who often lost at billiards, was bragging about being able to drive a car. His family owned the Grand Star Restaurant in Chinatown, and Frank was allowed to park the patron's cars. "Hey, I make good tip money!"

"I bet I could park cars, too, if anybody gave me a chance," joked Leighton.

"On weekends we have lots of people who come from all over with their cars. I dare you to come on over on Saturday to drive and park one of those cars. It's harder than you think. I'll check you out."

"Sure, I'll be there, but what will your mom and dad say?"

"They're busy inside the restaurant. We don't have to tell them anything until I know for sure whether you can handle those cars in the tight parking lot."

Leighton laughed, "Deal!"

The boys formed teams and spent the rest of the evening bowling against each other.

Early on Saturday morning, Leighton appeared at the Grand Star Restaurant. "Is Frank up yet?"

The waitress serving Dim Sum called toward the kitchen, "Hey Frank, one of your friends is asking for you."

Frank appeared, still a little sleepy-eyed. "Hey, Leighton. What's going on?"

"I'm ready to meet your challenge."

"Huh?"

"Remember, you dared me to come over to help you park cars."

"Man, I was just joking," Frank tried to wiggle out.

"I've been practicing with my dad's car, and I'd really like to get a chance to show you what I can do."

"Alright. Wait here and have some Dim Sum while I get ready," Frank and his family were known to be generous.

Leighton sipped on a cup of hot tea and enjoyed a few pot stickers, spring rolls and Siu Mai while he was waiting.

"Thanks Frank. I'm ready if you are," he said when Frank came back wearing his parking vest. He looked quite official with the yellow vest that had pockets for tips and tickets.

Leighton followed him out. When a customer drove up, Frank whispered, "Wait here, and watch me." Then he went to open the car door, "Allow me!" Handing the customer a ticket, he said, "Your car will be in Space number seventeen in that parking lot over there when you're ready to leave."

The man nodded and went inside.

Frank called Leighton to the car, "Okay get in. I'll drive this one to show you how we back into the space, so the customer can drive it straight out later."

Leighton watched Frank's feet operate the clutch, brake and accelerator pedals at the same time as concentrating on steering very carefully into the numbered space. "Let me try the next car. I think I can do that."

Frank was a little apprehensive. "Well, okay."

After Leighton had successfully parked five cars in a row, Frank became more confident. “I guess you’ll get your parking vest tomorrow. On Saturdays and Sundays, we start early. On Fridays we only need to work during the dinner hours. We work for tips. My parents don’t pay me for parking cars.”

“Got it, Man. Thanks a lot.” Leighton and Frank parked cars for the rest of the day. Tired but very satisfied, he left around eight in the evening, “See you tomorrow,” he waved and went home.

* * *

A few weeks later, Allen approached Leighton, “How come you always have money for movies and stuff?”

“I’m parking cars at the Grand Star Restaurant.”

“You what! Does Dad know?”

“No, I haven’t told him yet. He’s been pretty busy with his own job at the new Safeway. He’s one of their butchers and already got a raise.”

“Yeah, I knew he was good at his job, but I kinda wish he would talk more. He never wants to talk about Emily or Mom. Has he ever talked to you about where he was born or how he got to California?”

“No, I’ve asked him a couple of times, but he always changes the subject. One time I heard something about him buying his papers from another Chinese immigrant, but when I asked him about it, he told me to mind my own business.”

Allen nodded, “Yeah, that’s the same thing he told me. So that’s what I’m doing. I’m minding my own business.. The director at Echo Park takes me seriously and lets me use the equipment for free. I’ve even started to give tennis lessons for money.” Allen showed Leighton a few dollar bills. “Can you believe this?”

"Hey, we'll make it, you and I!"

"Did you hear about Uncle George?"

"You mean the one who got the Honorable Discharge from the army?" asked Allen.

"Yes. He went back to China to live with his wife right after that, but I heard that he brought his wife to San Francisco last month. They're living with Ted and working in his store."

"Ted? Another one of Mom's brothers?"

"No."

"This is getting too complicated for me," said Allen. "How do you know all this stuff?"

"Sometimes when we go to visit Mom, she tells me stuff."

"What kind of stuff? I thought she was crazy."

"No. She talks about her brothers and sisters, and how she came back from China and stuff," mumbled Leighton. "It's a long story. Maybe Dad thinks she's crazy, but I don't."

Allen started paying attention, "Well out with it. You got me all wondering now."

"Okay, you asked for it. You know that Mom was born in San Francisco, and she was taken back to China when she was only four and a half. Remember? You're the one who told me about Auntie Choy Ping. She's just a little older than Mom. There were four girls and two boys that our grandmother took back to China. They all grew up there, except Uncle Harry who was sent to Georgia to be raised by our grandfather's brother Kam Chen."

"Man, this really is complicated."

"Yes. Our grandfather had an Herbal shop in San Francisco Chinatown. Anyway, he sent his wife and six out of the seven kids to China. You already knew that, didn't you, Allen."

"Yeah."

"So now it's years later, and our grandmother had another son in China before she died in 1926. Mom and the little boy lived with a family in Canton. She took care of the boy and went to school there. A couple of years later Grandfather sent Uncle Harry who grew up in Augusta, Georgia, to China to find a wife. Uncle Harry stayed there a couple of years, but when he came back, he couldn't bring his young wife. There's a lot of complicated paperwork involved in bringing a wife, and I don't really know the details."

"Well, just tell me what you know," Allen was getting more and more curious.

"Instead of bringing his own wife, Harry was supposed to bring the wife and two sons of one of grandfather's cousins and his business partner to America. Their name was Wong, too. Well, Mom had just finished school. She was nineteen, and she knew that she was a United States citizen because she had some paperwork that said she was born here. She had saved up some money and somehow got all the documents ready in time to travel with Uncle Harry, and the Wong family. So there were five people who arrived in March 1930. Uncle Harry, Mom, Mrs. Wong (the distant cousin) and her two sons, Ted and Robert."

"Oh, so that's the Ted you were talking about."

"Yes, and that's the guy who owns a business in Oakland now. Uncle George recently brought his wife to America. He is working in Ted's store, and he's been writing letters to Mom and Dad. I think he wants to move to Los Angeles and work with Dad, but Dad doesn't own the store anymore."

"Dang, I didn't know any of this."

"I guess you should visit Mom once in a while. She's a lot smarter than Dad lets on. I still don't know why he keeps her in that stupid hospital." Leighton was visibly upset.

"Dad is Dad." Allen tried to calm him down. "It's hard to figure out what all he's gone through. He never talks about his feelings and memories."

"I know. I guess we'll just have to make the best of it."

Marianne

1947-1953

"Marianne, come sit over here, we have to talk," Tilly looked serious. Her visits had become fairly regular, and she always brought goodies that were hard to get in the small village of Macken. "There's something important happening in my life."

"What is it, Mutti? You're scaring me."

"I think I'm in love again."

"Oh good. I'm glad you and Vati are happy again. Where are we going to live? When are we moving?" A broad smile spread across the young girl's face. She had been telling Oma for months that she wished her parents would get together and come to live with her. She wanted to have a regular family.

Tilly realized what was in Marianne's heart. It was not going to be easy to convince the ten-year-old that a whole new life was awaiting her.

"No, your father and I are not getting along. In fact, that's what I wanted to tell you. We are getting divorced."

Marianne was stunned. "Divorced?" She had heard and read this word before, but she never thought it would happen to her own parents.

"Your Vati and I fight every time we see each other." Tilly turned to her mother, "Jakob is not a bad man, but the war has destroyed him. He doesn't love me anymore, and he only thinks of himself." Then she asked Marianne, "He doesn't even come visit you here in Macken, does he?" Tilly's voice began to shake, "I feel very bad for him. I think he has given up. All he does is feel sorry for himself in that little room of his."

"But Mutti, I thought you loved him. When we were in St. Wolfgang, you kept hoping that he would be alright. You always talked about him. You didn't want him to get killed in the war."

"Marianne things are different now. I don't love him anymore."

This conversation wasn't going at all the way Marianne expected. She thought her mother had come to visit with happy news, and now they were talking about stuff that made Marianne very unhappy.

"Mutti?"

"Yes?"

"What's so different? Can't we just try to live together and be happy?"

"No, it's too late. I've met a wonderful man in Frankfurt. That's the one I'm in love with."

Marianne felt her young heart tear into bits and pieces. She loved her mother and always wanted to make her happy. Her own happiness had always depended on her mother's. Now suddenly nothing made sense anymore. "Do I have to love this stranger, too? Are we moving to Frankfurt?" Tears were beginning to form.

"You'll like him. Just wait and see."

"But I love Vati." Crying now, Marianne looked at Oma, who looked shocked. "Oma, why?"

Her grandmother hugged the young girl who was crying her heart out. "Come, let's have some cake. I baked one of your favorites, Streußelkuchen (a crumb coffeecake) because I knew your mother was coming to visit."

As the three sat around the table, munching on the cake, Tilly and Oma discussed the new development that would change the family forever while the young girl tried to absorb these new and confusing words.

In her itinerant seamstress travels, Tilly had gone to Frankfurt to do some sewing for her childhood friend Hella who was now working in the Rhein-Main Air Force Base Exchange for the American occupation forces. Traveling between the American Zone and the French Zone was complicated and required special passes that included authorizations to work and travel. Tilly gladly endured many delays and inconveniences in order to visit her little daughter.

She also smuggled as much coffee, tobacco and soap as she could carry despite the strict inspections on the trains from one Occupation Zone to another.

"Mother, I was going to bring a box of cigars for Vatter, but the inspectors caught me, so they took it. I guess they were so happy with the cigars that they forgot to inspect my other suitcase. That's how I got away with this can of coffee and the soap."

Both of the women laughed. "Well, Vatter will just have to smoke the tobacco he grows in the garden."

Marianne was still thinking about this stranger who was giving so much stuff to her mother. "Mutti, is that why you love this man? Because he gives you stuff?"

"Let me tell you about him. Hella and a couple of her friends took me to a party on the Air Force Base. There were lots of American soldiers and German girls. Everybody was enjoying the music and dancing. They were all talking in English, so I felt kind of left out. Then this friendly-looking guy walked up and asked in German whether he could join us at our table. He explained that he is an American who was born in Germany and moved to America with his parents when he was only a little boy. He was so talkative and friendly that I started to feel more comfortable. Then he asked me to dance with him. He was a wonderful dancer, and pretty soon I forgot all the bad things that had happened to me because of the war."

"Mutti, is that when you forgot about Vati?"

"I guess so. Later I told him that I was divorcing and had a daughter. He told me he didn't mind. He asked me where I was staying in Frankfurt, so I told him I was just visiting Hella. I didn't think he would remember me, but the next weekend he came to

Hella's apartment and asked for me. I guess he had asked Hella for the address. He wanted to invite me to come dance again. He even gave me some cigarettes and a Hershey's chocolate bar. I wanted to say no, but I just couldn't."

"Chocolate?"

"Yes, Marianne, real chocolate. I hadn't had any for ages. This American, who spoke German and brought me presents and treated me like a lady, was like an angel from heaven."

Oma interrupted, "Tilly, you're crazy. This American is going to take advantage of you and then leave you when he goes back to America. Don't get all kinds of ideas about him. You'll get hurt in the end. Is this the reason for divorcing Jakob?"

"No, Mother. Jakob and I had our troubles even before the war. Now that times are so tough and everything is so scarce, our relationship has gotten much worse. Our marriage is over whether I have fun with this American or not."

"Are you thinking of getting married to him? What's his name? You haven't even told us his name yet."

"John."

* * *

In 1947 Tilly and Jakob's divorce became final. They decided on a "No Fault" divorce with joint custody of their only child, Marianne.

During the ensuing two years Marianne got to meet John a few times. He was always able to make her mother happy. That was the main reason Marianne warmed up to him. She didn't care about the gifts he brought, although he included the entire family in his generosity. There were always plenty of cigarettes, coffee and many other things that were not available in German stores.

In 1949 Tilly married John and emigrated from Germany. She left Marianne in Macken with her grandparents in the hope that she would eventually join her in America. The most significant complication was the joint custody both her parents had signed. Marianne's father was reluctant to sign the release papers for Marianne's emigration. After some bargaining via letters, he agreed to let Marianne leave Germany under certain conditions. He insisted that she would go to America on a ship rather than an airplane, that she was to write him at least one letter a month and that she would be raised in the Roman Catholic Church.

Eventually the arrangements were finalized, and a passport and a fully-paid ticket arrived in October 1950. Since Marianne was only thirteen years old at the time, arrangements were also made for her to be accompanied by a German couple who was emigrating.

By that time Marianne had become quite confident that she was equal to the adventure of going to America. Although she dreaded leaving her beloved grandparents, she eagerly counted the days until she could join her mother.

Her grandparents and friends were not quite so eager. The last few weeks in Germany became quite tense. Opa had become grumpy and drank more than ever. Marianne and her beloved Oma were constantly arguing. All three were on edge, and would rather have yelled at someone else than at each other. As the words, "Marianne is going to America" spread around the village, several villagers expressed their doubts. One old lady told Marianne in plain language that she would never see her mother again. Others warned her that she would never be happy in a foreign country. Others reminded her that it was the Americans who had bombed Germany.

A few, especially Herr Zensen, her enlightened teacher, and Pfarrer Andreas, the village priest, were more encouraging.

"If God wants you in America with your mother, you will get there," the priest told her. Herr Zensen reminded her that she was smart and could learn the English language very quickly. Marianne was going on simple faith. She was young and brave. She knew that her mother was already in America, that her father was finally willing to let her go, so that was that!

The day Marianne left the village, a large group of people gathered at the bus station to see her off. The priest, who had been her moral support and beloved mentor, was there offering his blessing and repeating his advice to have faith in herself. Her teacher had given her lots of advice, and her school friends, shouted encouragements as Marianne and her grandparents boarded the bus.

As the bus rumbled through the beautiful forests of the Hunsrück Mountains, Marianne waved good-bye to Macken and hello to Burgen where the train would take them to Koblenz. Marianne felt tremendously important. Somehow she sensed how much hope was pinned on her. She had been a child of the war. The villagers had nurtured her although they knew that she was not one of theirs and that she would leave one day. They had known what lay ahead, so they filled her with the wisdom that comes from living within the earth. She had been an alien, accepted with love, educated in their ways, and sent on her way into the greater universe to places with vaguely familiar names. The names of her destinations were the same names of the enemies who had destroyed so much of Germany. Would this child become one of them? Marianne's heart sensed her destiny. She was young, but she had read numerous books and was awed by the role she was chosen to play in the human drama.

They spent a few days in Koblenz saying goodbye to various friends and relatives. Suddenly it was time to go to the train station.

"Vati, why are we going to the train station? Am I going on a train? I thought I was going on a ship. The only ships in Koblenz are the ones on the Rhine River. Do they go all the way to America?"

"No, those are just river cargo ships."

"Am I going to go on a ship or not? I thought I was supposed to go on a ship to America." Marianne repeated as she was trying to imagine the great journey ahead of her.

"No. Let me explain. First Uncle Jupp and I are taking you on a train to Frankfurt where we will make sure you get on the right train to Genoa, Italy. Then you will ride on the train all the way to Genoa. You will even sleep on that train because it will take at least twenty-four hours…"

"Twenty-four hours! That a whole day and night! I don't like being on a train that long!" interrupted Marianne.

"Yes. You'll be fine. Tomorrow you'll arrive in Genoa. The train will travel through Switzerland during the night, and if you are still awake, you will see the Alps."

"St. Wolfgang was in the Alps. Will I see St. Wolfgang from the train?"

"No. it's too far away, but the train will travel through Lucerne and maybe Zurich."

"That's a long time. What if I get hungry?"

"Marianne, the ticket you have says that everything is paid for. You can eat in the dining car on the train. Also when you get to

Genoa, a man from the Red Cross will pick you up at the train station and take you to a hotel. That's where you will sleep and eat until the next day. Everything is paid for. The man from the Red Cross will have a badge, so be sure to check."

"Yes Vati, I'll be careful." Marianne pretended to be brave, but it wasn't working. She looked around searching the gathering crowd in the station. "Where are those married people that were supposed to go with me?"

"Marianne, listen carefully. That couple did not get permission to go to America because they haven't been denazified yet. You will have to make this trip without them." Jakob's voice faltered. He was terrified for his daughter and wanted to withdraw his permission for her trip, but he was committed to his promise. "Do you think you can do this, Marianne?"

"All by myself? I can't even speak Italian or English! I'm scared, but I want to go to my mother. I wish someone would go with me."

"You are thirteen and a half. That's old enough to know what you really want. I'm leaving it up to you. We can cancel the trip if you want." Jakob had composed himself.

"If I change my mind now and go back to Macken, all the people will laugh at me!" Marianne was torn. The moment of truth was hitting her hard, and a couple of tears rolled down her cheek.

Uncle Jupp had been watching this exchange. He had seen how brave Marianne had been on the trip back to Koblenz from St. Wolfgang. He looked directly at the shaking young girl, "Marianne, your mother will be waiting for you in New York. You are a very brave girl. Think of all the things you've already survived and accomplished. I'm sure you will get to America and your mother."

Jakob nodded. "Yes. Oh, I have something for you. I want you to have this watch. Knowing what time it is, is very important. Also, here is a twenty dollar bill. It is American money that can be spent anywhere in the world. It's not very much, so you'll have to be very frugal. Don't just spend it foolishly."

Marianne brightened up. "I won't Vati. You said that everything was already paid for. I'll just show them my ticket if they want money."

Both men laughed. They were sure that Marianne would be just fine. Uncle Jupp reminded her to keep her passport and ticket safe in the backpack. "Oma told me that she sewed a pocket into your underwear, too. That's for the money."

"Yes Uncle Jupp."

Secretly, Marianne was relieved that she would not have to answer to strangers for her every move. She almost welcomed the opportunity to assert her own maturity. How many children get the chance to step into adulthood in such a gloriously independent manner?

The family group stood around awkwardly in the large echoing train station. Each one was trying to make sense out of the situation. Grandfather "Opa" was offering last minute tips on how to deal with strangers. Grandmother "Oma" gruffly tried to shut him up while Uncle Jupp and Vati took care of the luggage. Their nervousness made Marianne strangely apprehensive, and she had moments of wanting to throw herself against them and beg them to take her back to Macken. Visions of her mother and a future stepfather confused her, so she was grateful for the matter-of-fact voice loudly announcing the departure of the train to Frankfurt over the loudspeaker. The world apparently cared little about a girl's confusion and was willing to accept her as a full-fledged traveler.

With Koblenz fast disappearing and Frankfurt materializing as her next goal, Marianne became clear-headed again. She busied herself with the details of the impending journey. She still had the two strong men at her side. Although Vati and Uncle Jupp were supportive, they were subdued. They listened in awe while Marianne chattered on about all the things she would see and experience between Frankfurt and New York. They had never sailed the oceans themselves and couldn't deny her childish ramblings, but they must have sensed their roles in a greater drama. After all, they were sending a thirteen-year-old girl into the world alone!

Arrival in Frankfurt was relatively uneventful. They stopped in the depot snack bar to eat a Bratwurst and play the "Groschenmaschinen" which were the popular slot machines of Germany. Marianne was, of course, quite excited and eager to get on with her adventure and had little time for caring about the feelings of her uncle and her father. They already seemed part of another world which Marianne was rapidly leaving behind, and she became less and less conscious of their existence. Finally it was time to board the train which would take her to Genoa, Italy for the next leg of her journey.

After all kinds of last minute instructions, including her father's short lesson on bartering with souvenir vendors instead of paying their marked prices, Marianne climbed into the waiting train. She double-checked her belongings. She had taken everyone's warning that people would try to steal her things very seriously. Her grandmother had known just how to fortify Marianne with the knowledge that no one could get at the treasures without her consent. Sewn into her underwear, a little pocket hid her money from the ever-grasping world. One suitcase packed with clothes and a few presents for her mother from well-wishers and one backpack with items she might need on the trip, plus the accordion case carrying her most precious possession, a 12-bass Hohner accordion, made up the bulk of her baggage. The backpack also contained a roll of cookies from a friend. As she clutched all her earthly goods and took mental inventory over and over again, she was overwhelmed by the great cacophony of whistles, loud voices, a crackling loudspeaker and conductors slamming the compartments shut. Marianne was on her way! A quick look out of the window confirmed the departure. The familiar but worried faces of her father and her uncle blended into the crowd left behind on the platform. Soon her heart beat in unison with the clickety-clack of the moving train.

As the train rolled comfortably through Switzerland toward the destination in Italy, Marianne began to get hungry and nibbled on the delicious cookies. She knew that her meal in the dining car had been paid in advance, but her fear of leaving her baggage unattended caused her to remain steadfastly in her seat.

"Come on, young lady. It's dinner time in the dining car." A kindly-looking conductor reminded her. "Your things will be fine here." But Marianne didn't trust him. She had been warned about kindly-looking people who cheat travelers and had no intention of being duped. She quieted her rumbling stomach with another cookie which didn't taste quite as good as before. The importance of keeping her possessions safe, made her discomfort a trivial nuisance, so she thought no more about it.

Toward nightfall, after another ticket and passport check, the conductor reminded her that she was entitled to sleep in the compartment just behind the seat. This was welcome news. She took all her luggage into the compartment and locked the door to keep would-be thieves out. Her exhaustion and the rhythmic clickety-clack soon lulled her to sleep.

The next morning, Marianne awoke with a terrible taste in her mouth. Eating only a few miserable cookies the previous day had done nothing for her breath, so she eagerly began to wash up and brush her teeth. Her morning toilette was nearly complete when she discovered that she had brought neither a hairbrush nor a comb. She searched through the back pack in vain. She looked in the mirror and thought, "*A young woman on an international voyage can't be seen in public with disheveled hair, could she*?" She thought about that problem for a while and came up with the brilliant idea of using her toothbrush to do her hair. She was quite pleased with the result and smugly stepped into the crowded passenger compartment, confident about her appearance.

If she had only been that confident about going to the dining car! It became more and more difficult to ignore the pleading of her stomach, but she was not yet ready to yield. She forced down a disgusting cookie.

Soon her attention was distracted again, however. Two ladies, speaking Italian, seemed very curious about this young girl traveling alone. They tried to ask her some questions. Speaking only German, Marianne couldn't engage in a lengthy conversation, but she understood the gist of their curiosity. With much hand-waving, pointing at signs and reading tickets, they suddenly discovered that Marianne was on the wrong train!

"*What am I going to do? What if I miss my ship? No! This can't be happening!*" The panic welling up inside her became a monster. The conductor was called. He did his best to reassure her that it was not too late to get to Genoa on time.

"We are going to make a stop in Milano. If we are lucky the train to Genoa will still be in the station," he smiled, "You can board it in plenty of time." Marianne dared not think about what would happen if the train had already left.

"If we are lucky?" Marianne got very suspicious. "What do you mean 'If we are lucky.' Don't you people know about your train schedules?"

The conductor smiled.

As they pulled into the train station, the conductor showed her the train one platform over. He and the two women were almost as relieved as Marianne was. Hurriedly, her luggage was placed on a porter's cart. A few Italian words were exchanged, and she followed the porter towards the other train. The porter managed to get the luggage aboard but refused to let her climb into the train. He held out his hand. She was confused for a moment but soon realized that he wanted money. She showed him her ticket, but he just shook his head. Several conductors on the platform were slamming the compartment doors shut. Marianne screamed, "I have no money. I need to get on the train! I'm going to America!" The porter kept holding out his greedy hand. Rather than let a little girl go, this man made Marianne go to a money exchange window for his tip! She was stunned. What if the train left with her luggage while she was trying to exchange the dollars into the Italian money? Rushing around in a panic, she somehow managed to exchange some of the dollars into Italian Lire and pay him, but she insisted on getting at least fifteen dollars in American money back. She looked at the five dollars' worth of Italian money. She grudgingly handed three hundred Lire to the porter who scurried off. Out of breath, she boarded the train just as it began to pull away.

Relieved, she fell into an empty seat next to an elderly man. She looked at the two kinds of money in her hand. "Vati told me that dollars can be spent anywhere in the world, but that lire are only good in Italy," she mumbled under her breath. As soon as the man heard her speak, he identified himself as a German. He calmly assured her that she was right about the money and that this train was indeed headed to Genoa. "Are you really traveling alone?"

"Yes, my father put me on the train in Frankfurt, and my mother will pick me up in New York.," she declared matter-of-factly without thinking of all the things that might happen in-between. He was astounded at her courage and wished her lots of luck. Then they fell into a pleasant conversation.

About two hours later the conductor yelled, "Genoa." Marianne's heart jumped. "This is it! Thank you for the nice talk. It helped to make the time pass."

She dragged her luggage onto the platform and just stood there for a moment. She was looking for a man with a Red Cross badge.

Suddenly, she felt someone grab her suitcase. She yelled, "Nein!" (No!) It was a porter trying to help her with the luggage. "No way! I remember what happened in Milano. I don't have that kind of money." She had been strong enough to carry her own stuff before, and she was not going to spend any more money on unfriendly porters. They were still struggling over the luggage when the Red Cross guy arrived.

He spoke in German. "What's going on here?" Impatiently, he listened to her story. Then he grabbed the suitcase handle out of the porter's hand and gruffly told Marianne, "Follow me."

A taxi took them through some cheerless streets before they stopped in front of a small run-down hotel. Pretentiously, this non-descript building called itself "Hotel Ristorante Firenze." In the lobby, Marianne had to engage in another struggle. After inspecting her ticket and her passport, the manager handed back the ticket but refused to return her passport. "I'm not allowed to let you keep my passport, please give it back," Marianne tried to remain friendly and calm.

The man with the Red Cross badge said, "That's the way we do things here. He will give the passport back to you tomorrow morning. Please follow the rules."

"But I have to go shopping. I need a hairbrush. I can't walk around Italy without my passport. I'm also very hungry!"

"There is a flea market just down the street. You don't need a passport to walk there if you come right back," he explained. "Now, let's get you settled into your room." They followed the manager up the stairs.

Shock!

"What!?! Am I supposed to sleep in here? It's a bathroom!" Marianne yelled as the door opened.

"This is the only room we have left, young lady. We put a cot next to the bathtub for you. You can lock the door from the inside, and no one will bother you." The manager assured her.

The Red Cross guy seemed very impatient with Marianne, "Stop making trouble, young lady. No need to yell."

So, here she was, a world traveler and adventuress extra-ordinaire, expected to sleep in a bathroom in a dingy hotel in Italy! She knew she could manage for one night, so she accepted the key and decided to calm down. Her immediate need for food soon urged her to go back downstairs to talk to someone about getting a bite to eat.

They understood. The Italian meal, though served courteously, was not exactly suited to her German taste, but it filled a void. Her next problem was a little more complicated. Her grooming the next morning would suffer greatly unless she acquired a new toothbrush and a hairbrush. She somehow convinced a fellow guest to walk with her to the flea market she had noticed on the taxi ride from the train station. The brisk walk in the balmy Italian evening completely revived her sagging spirits. After using some of her Lire to purchase a few necessities, she regained the confidence and bravado to go on with her fantastic journey.

Back at the hotel she became a bit concerned. She looked the bathroom over very carefully. There seemed to be no rats, and it smelled pleasant. Sleep was unlikely that night, however. Her stomach began to hurt. Being used to doing her necessary business in an outhouse on a farm, Marianne was cautious about approaching indoor plumbing. It reminded her of some of the bomb shelters she had to endure when the bombs were falling on Koblenz. "Oh Koblenz! Oh Macken! I wish I were back there!" She suddenly missed her Oma and Opa and the cozy home and the delicious bread. She lay down on the cot for a brief cry which soon cleared her mind. These unpleasant sleeping arrangements nearly overwhelmed her, but a kindred soul in the building on the other side of the alley must have sensed her discomfort. A loud female voice kept her sane by serenading the world and Marianne with heart-searing renditions of "O Sole Mio" and a couple of other arias until three o'clock in the morning. She finally dozed off and awoke around seven to a bright new day.

Joyfully she got herself ready for breakfast. This was the day! The food was nice, but the bill next to the plate was not. They wanted 2000 Lire! That would take her entire supply of dollars! Her family had assured her that all expenses on the train and at the hotel were prepaid. The effect on Marianne of seeing this bill for "first-class" accommodations was immediate.

The cute little thirteen-year-old German girl was suddenly transformed into a raging lioness. "How dare you charge me for something that has already been paid for and was a miserable mess besides!?" She stormed to the manager's desk and threatened to call the police. He tried to calm her down but insisted that on getting paid, or she wouldn't get her passport back. By the time the man from the Red Cross came to escort her to the harbor and the waiting ship, the situation had deteriorated into loud name-calling. A small crowd had gathered to watch the melee.

Knowing that there was still plenty of time before the ship was to heave anchor, Marianne insisted that they clear up this misunderstanding at the American Consulate. The two men looked at each other in amazement. "How do you know about the American Consulate?"

"My mother and stepfather told me about it in a letter, and my father told me not to let anyone cheat me out of money. We're going to the Consulate! I want my passport!"

A puzzled taxi-driver took the angry threesome straight to the Consulate where the matter was quickly resolved. Marianne did not have to pay, and furthermore, the manager was to return her passport, so that she could get on with her trip. Marianne sensed that all three of them would be glad to get her out of Italy.

After picking up the rest of the luggage at the hotel, the man from the Red Cross, who had by now acquired a noticeably respectful attitude toward Marianne, accompanied her to the harbor and paid the taxi driver. He then took her to the check-in with profuse good wishes and a sigh of relief.

It wasn't long before she met several other Germans in the large waiting room who would also be traveling on the SS Italia. In 1950, Germany had no shipping, so those who wanted to go by sea had to sail via Italian liners. While waiting for the call to board ship, they solidified into a lively little group. Marianne was certainly happy to meet some other Germans even though she was presently talked out of some of her money by one of them.

One of the German ladies, Bertha, seemed quite distraught. She felt it absolutely necessary to make a phone call which would cost ten dollars that she allegedly didn't have. "I need to let my husband know that we will arrive in New York on November 14." Her story sounded so sincere that Marianne was willing to part with her only ten dollar bill in order to abate that poor lady's distress. For the rest of the trip, Bertha was eternally grateful to Marianne and missed no opportunity to praise her and do little favors. She was sure that because of Marianne, her American husband would be waiting in New York ready to welcome this bedraggled group of Germans into the promised land.

Without any guarantees that the world was round, Marianne embarked upon the open sea. She had read stories about Christopher Columbus being born in Genoa, sailing with three ships from Portugal, and eventually discovering America. Now she was ready to follow in his wake, so to speak. "Isn't this exciting?"

Annie Koch, one of the German ladies looked a bit skeptical, "Exciting? I don't know. I'm more scared than I am excited."

Marianne stared at her, "Didn't you already survive the air raids and the bombings? What's to be afraid of after that experience? We'll be sailing to America like Christopher Columbus!"

The whole group laughed out loud.

A shrill whistle called everyone to attention. Then a loudspeaker crackled some Italian and some English into the atmosphere. Annie said, "I think they said it was time to board the ship. I'm so nervous!"

Several stewards lined up on the gangway welcomed everyone aboard the ship. After careful examination of Marianne's paperwork, one of the stewards escorted her to her cabin. Down, down into the ship they went. Steep metal stairs. No windows. Suddenly, she knew what Annie was saying about being scared. The resemblance to some of the bomb shelters she had experienced only a few years earlier weakened Marianne's knees. "*I'm going to America. I'll soon be with my mother.*" The steward was amused by her mumbling effort to comfort herself. He was just doing his job; she was risking her life!

The cabin was just large enough for four bunks with a narrow passage between them. There were also some lockers on each side of the door. One lady, already sitting on one of the bunks said, "You can take the top right bunk. The two bottom bunks have already been taken by our two other roommates." Marianne was surprised that no one was making a big deal out of her being an unaccompanied child. The steward matter-of-factly showed her the shower facilities. He also pointed to a sign which indicated in several languages, including German, that the water in this facility was saltwater and not potable. Only the faucet in the sink had fresh water. After leaving this pleasurable little place, they continued on their tour of the ship. Wearing her precious backpack, Marianne followed him like a lamb being led to the slaughter although she felt a thrill welling up deep inside. This was not a dream of going to America; this was the real thing!

Chattering continuously, she followed the steward across decks and up and down hallways. She was getting into the swing of the ocean voyage until they got to an opening from which emanated a loud mechanical clatter. It immediately became clear to her that this was only the way to the dining room. Through the opening, Marianne saw a catwalk, a very narrow hanging bridge above a spacious area full of engines. The space below was an engine room! From the years of thunderous air-raids and cage-like bomb shelters, Marianne had become fearful of all metal things that made noise and avoided them despite their peaceful purposes. She hesitated. Her elation had stopped at the sight and sound of the loud machinery just below her. She imagined it grinding her to bits if she lost her footing, or if the catwalk should suddenly collapse. The thought of having to walk back and forth across this abyss for every meal made her nauseous. She looked helplessly at the steward, "Is this the only way to get to the dining room?"

Surprisingly he answered sternly in German, "Yes, and if you want to eat, you will have to walk across this bridge. You are traveling in Cabin Class, and you may not go to the other parts of the ship unless one of the First Class passengers invites you."

Seeing the pitiful expression on the girl's face, the steward relented and smiled. He offered to hold her hand as he led the way over the menace. Another door or two, and the scene changed again. Now she was in an elegant dining room with tablecloths and flowers. Some people were already sitting at tables engaged in pleasant conversations. These people appeared unconcerned, so the memory of that fearful walk quickly faded. She heard happy voices and smelled the food. The steward showed her to a table and then excused himself. Soon she was nibbling on her first shipboard meal with a couple of friendly-looking strangers. There was no German bread or potatoes, but for a hungry girl there was enough to live on. She would deal with getting back to the cabin later.

When she was finished with her meal, she cautiously made her way back to the cabin. After making sure that her luggage was still intact, she decided to go back on deck. The ship had already moved away from the pier and begun its voyage. They were sailing on the Mediterranean Sea, and Genoa was slowly fading into the distance. Marianne looked around at the other people on the deck. Even though she didn't see a single familiar soul, she felt quite comfortable among her fellow human beings. This would be a common adventure! "*Come what may, for the next two weeks, all we have is this ship to carry us to the promised land,*" she thought. Most of the people were speaking Italian or English, but that didn't worry her. She had a place to sleep, eat and get cleaned up. *"I think I'll go down and take care of my luggage and hang up my clothes. I hope nobody stole my accordion."* She was making a plan for next two weeks.

Suddenly she saw the lady who had borrowed the ten dollars on the pier in Genoa. Bertha was speaking German to another young woman. Nonchalantly, Marianne joined them, and then Annie walked up, too. "Do you know that there are about a dozen other Germans aboard the ship? This is good news! Some of them even speak a little Italian or English to help translate, if necessary. This trip will be fun and exciting, after all."

"I told you so, Annie!"

A scheduled stop at Naples for several hours was too valuable to waste time on a ship. A few friends were making plans to tour the city and invited Marianne to join them. She asked, "Is this going to cost any money? We're all quite poor."

"Let's just walk around and see what there is," suggested Annie Koch.

As the group of seven debarked, posters next to taxi drivers offered rides around town for "one American Dollar, that's all." One of the taxi drivers gestured that he would let all seven ride for only six dollars. They looked at each other and decided to take a chance.

With great bravado, Marianne pointed at the sign and shook her head vigorously. She tried to make him understand, "No, too much! We want a bigger discount for the seven of us in one taxi. It will be very crowded!" He smiled and wrote a big five on a piece of paper. Marianne grabbed the pencil out of his hand, crossed out the five and wrote a four. He threw his hands in the air and then with a big grin let us climb into his cab. Marianne collected a few coins from each and paid the man.

Annie whispered, "How did you learn that?"

Marianne whispered back, "My Vati told me that Italians like to haggle. They won't respect people who pay too much, so I thought I would try it. It worked."

One of the stops on this one-hour tour of Naples provided a view of Mt. Vesuvius, an active volcano. A street photographer took a group picture. Here was another opportunity for Marianne to haggle! Again, she proved that her father's advice not to pay the full asking price to street vendors in Italy was true. The other ladies just let her take charge, and she was gaining confidence by leaps and bounds. Marianne had left her sheltered life in Germany only three days earlier, and already she felt like a seasoned world traveler. Shortly after returning to the ship, they set sail for the next day's stop, Rome.

It was announced that there would not be enough time in Rome for sight-seeing, so no one planned to get off the ship. The ship appeared to become more crowded. From her perch on the deck, Marianne was able to watch the new passengers walk up the gangway. None of the people who boarded in Naples and Rome were German. An American family with children came aboard, and Marianne noticed that several boys and girls her own age came to the dining room that evening.

The next day the ship made a short stop at Palermo, Sicily. Marianne walked down to the pier briefly to look what the vendors had to offer. She bought a white pearl rosary in a little metal box shaped like a bible for fifty cents. Her money was dwindling, but there would be no need for money once they began the actual crossing of the Atlantic Ocean. As of this moment, they had not yet left the sight of land. The ship had been traveling down the length of Italy, and now it was about to pass through the straits of Gibraltar. *"Gibraltar! I can't wait to see the Rock of Gibraltar in person."*

Throughout the years with her grandparents, Marianne had spent countless hours studying the few books they owned. There was a Holy Bible, a beautifully illustrated, leather-bound version of "Arabian Nights," a set of outdated almanacs, and a World Atlas. A few children's books and some movie magazines completed the collection. For years Marianne had memorized exotic names and geographic outlines and imagined herself traveling the world a thousand times. *"I can't wait to actually get to see the Rock of Gibraltar in person."*

It was twilight. The waves welled up higher and higher as the ship left the calm Mediterranean Sea and approached the Atlantic. Nothing deterred Marianne. Along with a dozen or so other brave (or foolish) souls, she stood awed in the bow of the ship. On the right, Gibraltar rose out of the water like a mighty fortress as the tiny ship sailed into the vast Atlantic Ocean darkness.

For an hour or so, Marianne stood mesmerized in the bow. She could not tear herself away despite the dark, damp cold. A salty wind whipped her hair and tore at her clothes, but she didn't care. She was immersed in a more important experience. There it was, no longer a flat outline on a paper map; she was looking at the real thing! Gradually, another thing that was real caught her attention.

She became aware of a yucky cold feeling creeping over her. She needed to take a warm shower and get the salt out of her hair.

It's a good thing that she continued to be thrilled about seeing Gibraltar because the shower proved to be a big disappointment. There was no hot water, so she had to shower in the cold saltwater. Fortunately, the sink had fresh water to rinse her hair. A couple of ladies took this opportunity to express their disapproval about wasting the fresh water meant for brushing their teeth. Feeling guilty as well as salty, Marianne crawled out of the bathroom like a whipped puppy. Annie met her in the hallway, “What is wrong, Marianne?”

“A lady yelled at me for rinsing my hair in the sink. She said I was wasting the fresh water.”

“Don’t worry, Marianne. The “first-class” passengers probably waste more than that just getting a drink.”

“Thanks, Annie. You’re a good friend.” Now I’m going to curl up on bunk and warm up for a few hours. Good Night.”

In the cabin, a strange sensation in the pit of her stomach suddenly came over her. At first she didn't understand it. She asked a cabin mate who explained, "We're sailing on the Atlantic Ocean now, and this is November. The ocean is not as calm as the Mediterranean Sea. The ship is moving up and down with waves, and you are getting sea-sick." She was right, but Marianne was tired enough to get a bit of rest that night. The next morning, she was barely able to nibble on an orange or a hard dinner roll that evening. Anything else threatened to come right back up.

As the ship approached Lisbon, Portugal, people cheered at the chance to walk on solid land again. The loudspeaker promised nearly six hours before leaving Lisbon, so there would be time to take a walking tour around the city. The little German group decided to look for some souvenirs shops along the waterfront. It was a beautiful sunny day, and the city was very clean. Vendors, offering items for sale, had set up their booths right on the pier. Marianne looked forward to the challenge of bartering for another "bargain." She saw a straw hat costing ten American dollars which she bought for three. She also bought a pair of little handmade dolls in Portuguese costumes after haggling for a much lower price. Marianne's friends just shook their heads and smiled.

Back on the ship, Marianne no longer felt queasy. In fact, she was getting quite comfortable as everyone settled in for the uninterrupted ocean crossing. In quietly exploring the various restricted areas of the ship, she discovered a game room where she saw the American boys and girls play cards. She tentatively approached them and heard them speak English as they played their game. One of the girls recognized her. "Didn't we see you in the dining room?" The two girls smiled, but didn't understand the words. Marianne took her small German-English dictionary out of her pocket, and communication was established.

With gestures and very few words, they invited her to play. She knew how to play cards because Opa had taught her many games, but she wasn't familiar with the game they were playing. "This game is called Canasta. Look, it's easy." They took time to teach her. It was the first time Marianne realized that learning something had nothing to do with the different languages people use. She was pleased to discover that people were able to communicate very well in other ways as long as they had a few tools and the will to use them.

One of the girls pointed at her watch, "Tomorrow, same time? Canasta. Here." Marianne nodded happily. They met several times throughout the trip to spend an afternoon playing Canasta. The one thing that Marianne regretted was that she could not afford to buy a drink at the snack bar while the other kids had money for a soda. While meals, including a beverage were included in the dining room fare, drinks in the game room were not. She had already spent almost all her money.

One of the attractions on deck was the sighting of whole schools of dolphins. Within picture-taking range of the ship, about twenty or thirty big creatures would arch out of the water gracefully and dive in again. People on deck went, "Oooh! Aaah!" at the sight. None of her relatives in Germany had thought of giving Marianne a camera for this momentous journey, but her mind's eye recalled the thrilling sight for years to come. Several times the dolphins put on the show for the passengers as the ship sailed through their domain.

Another show she enjoyed aboard the S.S. Italia was the movie, “I'll Get By,” It was the first Technicolor American movie Marianne had ever seen. She especially loved the music and the message.

Gradually, she became accustomed to the heaving and rolling of the ship. In the daytime she walked with confidence on the deck and was able to tolerate the strange Italian food even though her entire being craved the familiar taste of Oma’s home-made German bread. Despite looking forward to her new life in America with her mother, she began to miss the life she had so eagerly left behind. Visions of her grandmother crying and her grandfather making toys for somebody else made her heart ache. After each good cry, she played the accordion or took out her doll to find some comfort in familiar things. The nights seemed interminable. In the tiny cabin with three other people, she couldn't do anything but be quiet. Doubts began to creep into her thoughts of the past and the future, "*Did my family in Germany stop loving me when I left? Will my mother really be waiting for me when I get to New York?*" Sleep salted with tears brought some relief until the light of day invigorated her once again.

One morning at breakfast, she mentioned that she had an accordion. Annie asked, "Can you play?"

"Not very well. I haven't had enough lessons, but my Opa showed me how to play 'Waldeslust.' I can play a couple of other songs, but I make lots of mistakes."

"I have an idea. Bring your accordion on deck. Sometimes it gets very boring. Even if you make a few booboos, we'll still enjoy the music," Annie suggested. Bertha agreed.

"I'm too embarrassed to play in front of people," argued Marianne.

"You! Embarrassed? You can't make me believe that!" laughed Annie. "You would fight with the devil himself. Just try it, and see what happens."

So, music after breakfast, cards after lunch and a movie after dinner. The pleasant routine made the long days on the Atlantic Ocean go by.

The landing in New York was scheduled for November 14. The ship would be passing the statue of Liberty at five o'clock in the morning. Marianne had every intention of getting up early enough to witness the dramatic entry into the New World, but by the time she and Annie got on deck, the ship had already passed the landmark. It was a very foggy morning, so Annie rationalized, "We're too far away, and the statue would probably have been very difficult to see through the fog, anyway." As the sky-line of New York City grew more distinct, Marianne's heart wanted to jump out of her body.

"Mutti, Mutti!" she screamed when she noticed her mother's beautiful face in the crowd on the covered pier. There she was, watching her daughter's wild waving. They couldn't hear each other, so they just took in the chaotic scene of a ship's arrival. They both knew that it would take another hour or more before Marianne could get off the ship. Also everyone had to go through customs. Now that the ship was docked, and Marianne was looking directly at America and her mother, she could be patient. "*Nothing matters now,*" she thought. "*I can see my mother over there.*"

Nothing mattered. She had arrived.

After walking down the gangway with all her belongings, she had to go into a very large hall to place everything on a long table for the customs inspection. A mean-looking man ordered her to open her suitcase and the accordion case. He also checked the backpack. He barely gave Marianne enough time to hug her mother who was timidly standing by.

Speaking in German, Marianne asked, "Where's Daddy? Is he waiting for us?"

Tilly explained, "Daddy had to work, so his parents offered to drive their brand-new Packard to pick you up."

Marianne became curious, "His parents? Will they be my grandparents?"

"Yes, they are very nice people. I know that they will never take the place of Oma and Opa, but you will like them. You can call them Grandpa and Grandma."

"I miss Oma and Opa already, Mutti."

Just then the inspector interrupted the conversation. "Stop talking, or speak English!" Marianne suddenly became afraid without knowing why and clung to her mother. “What’s the matter with his man? Why is he so unfriendly?”

“Shh! Marianne, don’t make a fuss.”

Marianne was puzzled. Why did her mother act so scared. During the war she had always been so brave. “Mutti, what’s wrong?”

Tilly half whispered, “He is part of the government. He’s an inspector! And he could make lots of trouble for us.”

Tilly’s apparent fear of officials still had an effect on her even in this free country. This didn’t make sense to Marianne. She had been told that America was a free country, where things were wonderful and people were friendly, but now she sensed that mean people could be anywhere. After looking through all the luggage, the man yelled something in English at my mother. She turned nervously to Marianne and explained, “You’ll have to give up your accordion.

A scream escaped Marianne’s open mouth, "Why?”

Tilly and the inspector looked surprised at the girl.

“Mutti! You gave me this accordion. You even made someone a dress to get this accordion. He can’t take it away!" Marianne stammered through her indignation.

"During the war, the Hohner Company which made this accordion has also been involved in building weapons for Hitler's army," Tilly tried to explain. "The American government won't let any of this company's products into the country. You'll have to give up this accordion."

Now the screaming started in earnest. At first Marianne yelled all kinds of German at him. When he didn't understand, she lost all control. She grabbed the accordion and put up such a ruckus that people started gathering to watch. Another customs agent came over to whisper something in the mean one's ear. Finally he relented, "Okay, then let me have this crystal butter dish, and you can keep your accordion."

Marianne who had already composed herself after yet another battle with an authority, spoke up, "This butter dish is a gift for my mother from her mother, my Oma. What are you going to do with it?" She was reluctant to let it go to this brutish man, but he was adamant. Either the butter dish or the accordion had to be sacrificed to the U.S. government. Marianne's mother timidly handed the crystal over. Marianne was outraged.

Just then Bertha who had borrowed ten dollars from Marianne in Genoa came running toward them. "Here's your money. Thank you so much for helping me. Because of your kindness, my husband was waiting for me right here in New York." Marianne's mother looked puzzled. After the lady explained the story to her, she took a long look at Marianne, "You are really something. I'm going to enjoy getting to know you as a mother should know her daughter. Welcome to America."

* * *

In the soft backseat of the undulating Packard on the way to Iowa Marianne's mother filled her ears with fantasies. "We have a nice new apartment. You will have your own room in our new apartment. You'll be going to a Catholic school. I already met the very nice nun who will be your teacher. You're going to love America."

"I don't feel good, Mutti."

Tilly kept talking. "We're selling the mobile home because you should have your own room." She talked of her wonderful husband. She talked of her new friends. Glowing reports. Blah, blah, blah. Marianne threw up. After the new grandparents cleaned up the backseat, they let her sit in the front seat for a while.

After her arrival, Marianne had to become a different person. She realized at once that she would have to change completely from that bold and adventurous young lady who had talked her way across an ocean, into a submissive child who had to obey her mother.

She knew that she no longer had the chance to fight it out with hotel managers, customs officers, or men from the Red Cross. Her mother did not want her to bother other people with family problems. Marianne was expected to blend into the mass of teenagers as soon as possible. A face in the crowd, so to speak. Not making waves.

Somehow she managed to accomplish this, but that accomplishment was actually the destruction of a very important part of Marianne. She became withdrawn and antisocial. It took years for her to overcome the culture shock completely.

Because of her extreme self-consciousness about the new words that came out of her mouth, Marianne spoke very little for nearly a year. As a result, her school work was excellent. That sounds contradictory, but it was true. She spent hours memorizing spelling words. At test time, she nearly always got 100%. Her math grades were also very good because mathematical symbols were identical in English and German. All her homework was on time, neat, and correct. Other subjects, such as art and science also required more written work and manual dexterity than social skills. There too, she got good grades. Her teacher, Sister Michaeline, praised her. She was learning English, the language of the angels.

Due to the strained relationship between Germany and America, Marianne realized that it was very important for her to become American and forget all things German. Not only were her German language skills useless in school but also her memories. Hitler and World War II were expected to disappear in the joyful abandon of the American way. Her experiences seemed to have no place or value in her new life.

* * *

Marianne's father had allowed her to emigrate with the stipulation that she was to write him at least one letter a month. This was a difficult promise to keep. Her German language was fading fast.

"Speak English! You're in America now!" was her stepfather's reminder whenever Marianne and her mother spoke in the familiar German. Except for the English-German dictionary, there was almost no German reading material in their home. At thirteen and a half Marianne worked diligently to catch up to the students who had been going to school uninterrupted from the time they were six years old. Her schooling in Germany had been sporadic: three weeks of grade one, two weeks of grade two, and practically none in grade three. Her grandparents had taught her as much as possible, and she was an avid reader, but her formal education had not started until she entered the fourth grade. As a result, she was barely able to put a proper German sentence together.

"Marianne, you have to write your father a letter. That was part of our agreement to get you over here." Her mother begged, "Please, just write a few words." She had shoved some stationery toward the pouting girl.

"Mutti, the last time I wrote him a letter, he answered my letter, but he criticized almost every word I had written. I can't stand to write German. I don't know how, and Vati is making me feel stupid. I'm studying English to please my American Dad and writing German to please my German father. It's just too hard to make you all happy and it feels like my brain is cramping!" she whined.

"Do what you want!" Her mother got angry and grabbed the paper away.

Marianne ran into her room to mope. "I wish I were back in Macken with Oma and Opa," she yelled as she slammed the door shut. Then she cried herself to sleep.

Letters to her grandparents and her father became rare. Eventually, Marianne stopped writing letters to Germany altogether despite the guilty feelings generated by that neglect.

Marianne wasn't particularly thrilled with her "own" room. Everything was strange, including the square ceiling light that cast mysterious shadows across the magazine pages she was trying to decipher. Even Christmas didn't do much to make her feel at home. Her new grandparents were friendly, but they could not take the place of her beloved Oma and Opa.

* * *

When, a couple of weeks after the holidays, Tilly and John took her to see their "trailer for sale" on the dealer's lot, she finally brightened up. This small home had no stone-like walls. There were lots of shiny wooden cabinets and windows. Instead of the wide open spaces of the hard, rectangular apartment, the wood-paneled trailer had cozy nooks and crannies where her spirit could feel safe. "Mutti, I like this. It's much better than the apartment. Do you have to sell it? Can't we live in this trailer?"

“John, let’s talk about this. I like the trailer better than the apartment, too.” We could move to the same trailer park where your parents live.” Tilly and Marianne talked John into giving up the apartment and moving back into the trailer. A spot in the trailer park was readied, and the small family moved in before the winter snows stopped.

For the first time since her arrival she began to look for friends her own age. Her school mates were friendly enough, but they all lived far away from the trailer park. Marianne made tentative steps toward Janice Shoemaker, a sixth grader who lived a couple of trailers down the road. Janice was happy when Marianne invited her to go roller skating, so John and Tilly drove them to the roller-skating rink on Saturdays. The two girls also enjoyed spending the twilight hours on the playground with the smaller kids who lived in the trailer park.

Marianne’s stepfather, John, now called “Daddy,” took her to school in the mornings, but getting home from school in the afternoons was an adventure in itself. Marianne had to catch a public bus at the school. Near the Post Office downtown, she had to get off and walk to the Recruiting Station in the huge Federal building where John worked. He had accepted an assignment as an Air Force Recruiting sergeant in order to provide some stability for his new family. For a couple of hours every afternoon, Marianne was allowed to sit behind one of the desks to do her homework. Three other military guys who were also working in the same Recruiting office, were always willing to help, so she learned English by leaps and bounds. It was quite a satisfactory arrangement for a couple of months. Then suddenly it was spring.

By May, Marianne had become familiar enough to ask her mother whether she could invite a few girls from school to help her celebrate her fourteenth birthday. After school, Daddy piled all six in the car and drove them to trailer park. It was obvious from their behavior that none of the girls had ever been in a trailer before. Marianne was so nervous she could have jumped out of her skin. Suddenly she became very much aware of the chasm that existed between these rich girls from good homes and herself, a poor girl living in a trailer. Bravely, she remained calm and enjoyed the party as much as possible.

For the eighth grade promotion ceremony the girls were expected to wear pastel colored dresses. Her mother made a lovely dress in a soft yellow with navy blue trim. A chic hat, a purse and some new shoes signaled that Marianne had grown up, but there were many more steps to take.

Between childhood and adulthood lies a "Losthood" for most children. Marianne's childhood had been chaotic, but she had survived. At the promotion ceremony from the small and protective Catholic school, she became apprehensive about another transition. Once again she was leaving a familiar scene and embarking on a journey into the unknown. How would she fare in a public high school with hundreds of students who spoke English?

Eventually she escaped into a familiar realm: books, magazines and especially comic books. She spent hours reading, in English, of course.

Franklin High School accepted Marianne because she had obviously learned enough English to predict her success in public schools. During summer vacation, another ninth grader, Faye Renner, had moved into the trailer park, and she also rode the school bus. The two girls became good friends immediately because they discovered lots of things they had in common despite their different backgrounds. Faye had played the clarinet in her junior high school band, and Marianne had a little experience on the accordion. They also discovered the joys of Monopoly and giggling about boys during the summer months. At school they ate lunch together and bolstered each other's spirits in the presence of a huge student body that did not seem to welcome newcomers.

Because teachers had trouble understanding her, Marianne was placed with a very friendly and effective speech therapist. She taught her how to roll the "r's," tongue the "th's," and differentiate between the German and English "w's." The therapist used the book about Squanto, the Iroquois Indian. She was going to speech therapy twice a week. At home she had a stack of comic books that kept her company when Faye was busy with her family. For a few hours each day Marianne remained in her own space. The argument about letter-writing became routine, but there was nothing to be done. Marianne's German was rapidly fading away into a hazy past.

Although Marianne was earning good grades in English, Math and Science, she was completely lost in History and Civics classes. From experience, she knew that the government of a country could wreak havoc upon the common people. In Civics, she was supposed to learn that government was based on an orderly set of checks and balances that allowed people to participate and vote. There was supposedly a U.S. Constitution that everybody followed. Marianne remained skeptical. Do the leaders of a country really follow a Constitution? Do people really have all the rights in the Bill of Rights? Never mind all the difficult English she had to translate; she simply couldn't believe the concepts of freedom in a constitutional government. Her German/English dictionary was not much help. Daddy had done his best to explain things to her on the way to school during the previous year, but she remained skeptical. He had discussed the Bill of Rights and he promised that the American Dream was real. "This country, unlike the Germany under Nazism, allows individuals to vote and make their own decisions."

* * *

"Daddy, they were talking about Korea in school today. Is there another war? I thought there weren't going to be any more wars."

"Well, it's very complicated. After the Second World War, the winners split up Korea, but the Koreans in the North attacked the Koreans in the South with the help of the Russians, so now we're helping the Koreans in the South. Don't worry, it has nothing to do with you. You're safe here in America," Jphn promised.

She believed him and ignored any news about wars and stuff like that. She had more pressing things to worry about.

* * *

Marianne earned an "A" in General Math the first semester, so the teacher recommended her to Algebra A for the second semester. Marianne earned another "A" and was very proud of her accomplishment. She wanted to get into Geometry in the tenth grade, so she had to take Algebra B in summer school. Up to that time she had never shared a classroom with a "colored person"; after all, it was 1951. Summer school turned out quite differently from what she had imagined. She thought she would actually learn Algebra B, but....

For six weeks that summer, she suffered through a noisy class at McKinley High School, which was located in a part of town she had never seen. "Colored people" lived there. Marianne was afraid. Nothing had prepared her for the gulf that existed between white and black Americans. The black girls, giggling in small groups, stared at her. Black boys made rude remarks. Even though there were a few other white students, there was no familiar face to make her feel safe. When Marianne expressed her concerns to John, he dismissed "those people" as trash. "Just get your Algebra credit, and don't worry about them," he advised.

Somehow Marianne got the credit for that class to make her eligible for Geometry in the tenth grade; however, she learned much more than just math. For the first time she learned about race relations in America. An uneasiness crept into her soul. Hadn't she already witnessed the unpleasant results of racial hatred?

The hectic life of a sophomore at Franklin High soon made her forget the other side of town. She continued to make academic progress but remained very shy in social contacts. She and Faye remained friends, and a few other girls were welcomed into their bond as well. Marianne, still mistrusting, discovered that she could ward off boys' friendly advances by averting her eyes. She averted her eyes a lot that year. Marianne had plenty of priorities before boys in her life.

* * *

For one thing, her family was about to grow. She would have loved a baby sister or brother, but she had to settle for an aunt. Tilly's sister, Leni, had survived the ravages of World War II in Berlin with a terrible burden of memories and deprivation. She had been a master beautician, but under the current economic stresses, she was unable to regain her balance. "Tante Leni" wanted to come to America, and Tilly wanted to make this possible. The trailer was barely big enough for three. "*Where is Tante Leni going to sleep*?"

"Your bed is big enough for two," said Mutti. "And you can give her two of the drawers in the dresser. You don't have that much stuff, so two drawers should be enough for you."

In December 1952 John drove the family to Chicago to pick up Leni at the O'Hare airport. Right away there was an argument between Tilly and Leni about money. Apparently, Leni had spent all the pocket money Tilly had sent her for the trip and requested more. The drive back to Cedar Rapids was not pleasant. Marianne was not too happy about having to share her bed, and Tilly was still upset about money. John tried to make light of having to "take care" of three women now. The tension level increased noticeably. Tilly became especially sensitive to Leni's chatter in German and expressed her desire for peace and quiet several times.

The family of four in that small trailer had practically no privacy. It became increasingly more difficult to find the time and space for Tilly's "peace and quiet" and Leni's strange habits. There was very little room for Leni and Tilly to write letters home, while Marianne was happy not to write anything! She had already learned that she would rather read than write. Reading, curled up in a corner somewhere, Marianne was comfortable and did not take up much space. "I'm glad you are writing letters to Germany. I really hate writing," declared Marianne frequently.

There was another stumbling block to acquiring writing skills: Typing Class. As an elective in the first semester of the tenth grade, Marianne chose Beginning Typing. She thought this would make writing easier since she had never developed good penmanship. She hoped that if she could see her words in print, they would look better and she would be more motivated to write those letters she owed her grandparents and her father in Germany. She was mistaken.

Typing class was very unpleasant. The typewriters clattered noisily into her sensitive ears, and the teacher was difficult to understand. Her fingers didn't want to cooperate, so the keys kept getting glommed up. Each key of a typewriter was attached to a lever with a raised letter that had to press against an ink-filled typewriter ribbon which then imprinted the letter on the paper. The levers got entangled in the center of the machine whenever the fingers accidentally pressed more than one key at a time. In the nervous effort to keep up with the speed tests, Marianne's fingers often pressed more than one key, and then she had to disentangle the levers. In the process she usually got some of the ink on her fingers, smudging the paper that was to be turned in. This class was sheer torture.

As a result of this torturous typing class and the forced letter-writing, Marianne developed a true antipathy against writing and only wrote just enough to graduate from high school. It would take years for her to change her attitude toward writing.

* * *

Four people in one thirty-foot house trailer were at least two too many. The three adults tried to improve their lives by spending a great deal of time at the VFW drinking their troubles away. Marianne began to dread their noisy return from partying on weekend nights, but she somehow managed to escape into her beloved world of reading.

She loved the comic books and the radio shows of the time. The Lone Ranger was her favorite! She listened to the Green Hornet, the Shadow, Sky King, Hopalong Cassidy and many others. The world of fantasy took her away from the harsh realities of the adult world.

* * *

The need for money pressed everyone into action. Encouraging Marianne to do well in school, Tilly and Leni worked at a molasses factory instead of going to adult school to learn English. When Marianne asked why they didn't work at their learned trades as seamstress and beautician, she was told that they didn't know enough English to get their required business licenses or be hired anywhere. They would have to work in a factory because they needed money and didn’t have time to go to school. Yet the reason they couldn't work at their learned trades was their incompetence in English. This seemed very unfair and illogical to Marianne, but the two sisters accepted their fates and enjoyed their jobs. Tilly was determined to get her citizenship papers. She studied privately with John without going to school, passed the test, and proudly received her Certificate of Citizenship. Leni attended evening classes at a local adult school.

One day John arrived with news. "I requested a transfer out of recruiting last month. Today I got the word that I'll be on active duty again."

He and Tilly had previously discussed his desire to get out of recruiting. Now Tilly was not so sure. "The Cedar Rapids Recruiting Office is a nice safe place to work. I don't want you to get transferred to Korea."

"I'm just getting very restless. I don't want to send young men into a war while I'm hiding out in an office job. The Air Force really needs my skills as a mechanic," John explained.

"So have they told you where they want you to go?"

"Yes, I've been transferred to George Air Force Base in Victorville, California, and we might be able to move into base housing after getting there. I'm still trying to decide whether we should pull the trailer or take the train to California."

"Well, it's up to you, John. None of us have a driver's license, so we won't be able to help. Whatever you decide is fine with me," said Tilly.

Tilly, Leni and Marianne wondered whether they were ready for the Wild West as they set out one February 1953 morning. Securing the breakable stuff but without having to pack up clothing and bedding, the family decided that it would be convenient to move their entire trailer home to Victorville. John bought a large Packard to pull the trailer. Marianne was excited. “We’re moving to California like Gypsies!”

In the Library

"Hi Randy, ready for another history lesson from an ole vet?"

"Do we have to?"

"No, but if you want to know more about how Leighton and Marianne go together, I have to tell you about the Korean War."

"We learned about the Korean War, but the teacher told us that it wasn't a war; it was a Police Action."

"Well, that's what President Truman called it, but it was a real war."

"You mean because of the killing?"

"Yes. Let me explain. Korea became a protectorate of the Japanese Empire with the Japan-Korea Treaty of 1905. Five years later, the Japan-Korea Treaty of 1910 set up the annexation of Korea, but the regent of Korea did not actually sign this treaty. Japanese Governor-Generals took over the administration of the Korea government, opening up economic opportunities for Japanese in Korea."

"Man, that's a long time ago. How come they started fighting forty years later?"

"Early in the twentieth century, Japanese farmers were encouraged to immigrate to Korea. Thousands of Japanese settlers established Japanese communities throughout the annexed country. Land reform with its new laws and restrictions allowed Japanese to become landowners. Korean farmers lost ownership of their lands; instead, they became tenant farmers who had to pay up to half their crops as taxes to the new government.

After World War I, many Koreans migrated to Japan looking for work. By the beginning of World War II, nearly a million Koreans had moved to Japan as laborers. When Japan increased its military forces for World War II, more laborers were needed to work in factories. By the end of World War II, more than two million Koreans lived in Japan, and nearly two hundred thousand Japanese lived in Korea."

"So everybody was happy?"

"Not exactly. At the end of World War II, it became the task of the United Nations to dissolve the Japanese Empire and repatriate the immigrants to their own countries, especially Korea. This proved to be a daunting task because of the strained relations between the USSR and the United States."

“What did the United States and Russia have to do with the stuff that was going on in Japan and Korea?”

“Despite their differences, the United States (US) and the Soviet Union (USSR) agreed on the surrender of Japanese forces in 1945 and divided up Korea along the 38th parallel. The North would be under Soviet occupation while the South would be under U.S. occupation.

A tentative truce between the two “Superpowers,” the US and the USSR, soon returned to the historical mistrust and even open hostilities. Raids by North Koreans across the 38th parallel, which had been set up as the “Demilitarized Zone,” (the DMZ) eventually led to more and more tensions. The Soviets with the support of Communist China supported the North Korean attacks, but withdrew its support and troops after an uprising in North Korea which killed more than 60,000 people in April 1948. In South Korea, suspected communist sympathizers were arrested or killed. While a war between North and South Korea was not supported by the US nor the USSR, the hostilities grew between the two parts of Korea. North Korea launched an invasion called “Fatherland Liberation War” June 25, 1950 with permission from Stalin, the Premier of the USSR.”

“Man, what is all this fightin’ and killin’ about, anyway?”

“Randy, that’s a great question! The truth is that I don’t know the real answer to that. I’m just telling you what happened not why it happened.”

“I understand, Joe.”

“The United Nations, led by the United States, supported South Korea. The UN had empowered the U.S. to select a commander, so the Joint Chiefs of Staff unanimously recommended General MacArthur who had been successful in World War II. China, assisted by the USSR, supported North Korea in the war that began to rage across Korea. Experienced Soviet generals and weapons left over from World War II were sent to North Korea.

The Korean War, which lasted until 1953, claimed many human lives and also contributed to the stand-off and arms race called the Cold War."

"The Cold War?"

"That what people in the press and in government called the time when the United States and the Soviet Union faced each other as enemies without actually bombing each other."

"Wait! I just remembered something from history class. The teacher was talking about proxy wars, where the superpowers got other countries to fight each other. That really sucks!"

"Randy! Even though you're probably right, I'd rather you didn't talk that way."

"Okay Joe, I'll dial it back, but you still haven't told me how the Korean War affected the lives of Marianne and Leighton. They were just teenagers then, going to school. Why should they worry about what was happening on the other side of the Earth?"

"Randy, they shouldn't, but even without knowing, they were affected in the way their lives turned out."

"See? That's how you snare me into listening to you!" moaned Randy.

"Come on, it's just getting interesting. Marianne moved to California with her U.S. Air Force stepfather who had decided to reenter active duty as an airplane engine mechanic rather than remain in the relatively safe recruiting job in Cedar Rapids, Iowa. He wanted to help fight against Communism."

"What about Leighton?" asked Randy.

"Living in Los Angeles, Leighton and many of his friends considered enlisting in the military because of the Korean War. Let me tell you how that worked out."

Leighton

1948-1951

Leighton and a number of his friends enrolled at Belmont High School in September 1948. He was not really looking forward to three more years of sitting in boring classes, but at least Math and Drafting would remain interesting. “Maybe we’ll meet even more friends,” he told Benny.

Allen had started at Belmont the year before, but he was running with a completely different crowd. His tennis skills had given him a reputation of being a “Jock.” He even played in the city tennis clubs and won a couple of tournaments.

Both boys stayed away from home as much as possible. The house was a wreck, and their father had become more and more withdrawn. Consequently, they earned their own pocket money and pursued their own interests. At night they returned home to do their laundry and get some sleep before the next day's activities.

* * *

"Hey, Leighton, we're going cruising after dinner. You wanna drive my car?" asked Benny during the lunch break.

"Sure, what time?"

"Stanley, Elmer and I are going to be at the bowling alley till five and grab something to eat there."

"Can you come pick me up afterwards? I don't like their food, so I'll fix something at home for myself." Leighton knew he had some homework to do before hanging out with his buddies, but he didn't want them to know that he was still trying to get good grades.

"Are you still parking cars at the Grand Star, Leighton?"

"Sure, it's good money on the weekends. I don't have to go downtown to shine shoes anymore," laughed Leighton. "I also got a day-time job at System Park downtown."

"Good thing, There aren't very many soldiers anymore, anyway," answered Benny.

"That's true. No more wars! People are starting to relax about that kind of stuff."

"Okay, see you later."

* * *

Leighton was driving down Pasadena Avenue in Pasadena with all the car windows open. He was trying to stay clear-headed while his four buddies were sharing tokes. Another car pulled up next to them at the intersection.

“Hey,” a rough-looking driver yelled at Leighton.

“What’s up?”

“My nieces here want to check you boys out,” the Mexican called into the car. “Stop in that parking lot over there.”

Leighton pulled into a parking lot, and the other car stopped right beside him. A couple of pretty girls got out and suggested, “Let’s drive around for a while.”

Norman and Benny opened the door and jumped out of the car. “Sure. We’ll ride in your car, and you can get in here. This is Elmer, and this is Stanley. They’re friendly and won’t bite. Leighton is our driver. You got another cousin for him?”

Another pretty girl got out of the car and got into the front seat next to Leighton. She smiled, “I guess we won’t be able to do much necking while you’re driving.”

“That’s right. It’s up to me to get you all home safely. Your uncle would have my neck if we got into an accident or anything bad happened to you.”

“That’s for sure,” she teased back.

Norman and Benny piled into the Mexican uncle’s car, “See you back here in an hour,” someone yelled as the car drove off.

The girl in the front seat turned the radio on, and Nat King Cole’s “Nature Boy” was playing.

One of the girls teased, “So, are you Chinese guys also nature boys?”

“Dang right!”

Leighton was trying to pay attention to the traffic while the heavy necking began in the back seat. The girl next to him moved closer and closer.

"Hey, let me park the car before you cause me to have an accident," Leighton smiled at the girl.

"Okay, okay. I was just thinking how good-looking you are."

"Thanks, but I really have to watch the road and the traffic."

* * *

"House party at Marlowe's next Saturday, think you can make it, Leighton?" The guys had gathered at the pool hall and were discussing their social life.

"I think so. Usually, most of the cars are parked by eight thirty or so. If you can come pick me up, Benny, I'll be ready."

Benny was very proud of his car, a 1949 Mercury convertible. He let Leighton drive it most of the time because Leighton was the one who stayed clear-headed. Most of the crowd enjoyed a toke while riding around, but Leighton had tried one once and didn't like the taste. He preferred to smoke Lucky Strikes.

When Benny and Leighton arrived at Marlowe's house, the music was already playing. Elmer met them at the door. "Good to see you make it. We've got cold beer waiting for you."

Nobody had invited any girls, so the guys just sat around listening to music and drinking beer. "That's a great car you've got there, Benny. How can you afford it?" Norman asked.

"Well, when my dad died, I inherited a bit of money. My mom works and earns enough to support the family, so I decided to buy a car."

"Dang, a Mercury. We ought to call ourselves the Sino-Mercs."

"Great name for our gang," agreed Marlowe.

Stanley argued, "Hey, it's Benny's car not ours."

Benny laughed, "As long as you guys chip in some gas money, I'll let you ride with me. And you can make up a name for our group."

The boys broke up the party around midnight, and everybody got home safely.

* * *

Most of the twenty-five members of the Sino-Mercs were Chinese, but there were also a couple of Japanese, Mexicans, Caucasians and Blacks. They were one of the more respected gangs at Belmont High because they didn't start any fights or harass anyone. Mostly, they just supported each other if one of them got harassed by someone else. Leighton, Norman, Benny, Tomlin, Frank, Roger, Myron, Elmer, Stanley, Wilson, Fred, Tommy, Wallace, Alfred, Ernie, Douglas, Donald, Edwin, Willie, Gene, and Sammy usually met at lunch. A few girls, Tomio, Tomoya, Irene and Lois, often joined them in easy-going get-togethers.

One day, a Japanese guy from another gang, approached a few of the Sino-Mercs. "You guys think you're so smug. I bet you'd flee like rats when the chips are down."

"Just because we don't cause any trouble, doesn't mean we're cowards," replied Alfred.

"Yeah. Let's meet at Scrivener's drive-in after dinner tonight and hash this out. We'll see who flees when the chips are down," said Norman.

Several of the Japanese guy's friends nodded. He said, "Fine, See you at Scrivener's at seven."

That evening the Sino-Mercs showed up in four cars in front of Scrivener's. Two or three guys from the other gang happened to be there.

"So where are your big-mouth friends?" asked Benny.

"Huh?"

Leighton explained, "Someone from your gang challenged us, so we're here."

One of the Japanese guys said, "We don't know anything about that."

The Sino-Mercs waited for a few minutes to see whether the guy who mouthed off would show up, but nobody did. "Come on," said Frank. "Let's go shoot some pool. Those guys with the big mouths were all talk and no action."

Leighton agreed, "They know we're united."

* * *

Most of the Sino-Merc guys had a particular girlfriend, but Leighton was a bit hesitant about committing to a relationship. Instead, he admired a few girls from a distance. Molly was one of his favorites, and he also spent some time with Lois and her sister Irene. When one of his classmates, Carolyn, said that she was going to summer school, Leighton told her that he was also going to try making up some credits toward graduation.

"Maybe, I could pick you up and drive you to school if Benny lets me use his car."

"That would be great, Leighton," Carolyn agreed.

Benny trusted Leighton with his car. "Hey, Leighton, we're brothers, ain't we?"

That summer, Leighton got acquainted with Carolyn's parents, and they trusted him to take care of their daughter. He did keep her safe and they talked about a lot of things, but there was no romantic spark.

Shortly after the new school year started in September 1950, Leighton was already bored. Prior to his senior year he was on track to graduate after the first semester. His all-knowing seventeen-year-old attitude had lost all interest in passing the few classes he still had to attend. His brother Allen had enlisted in the Marines in June right after the Korean War started. "What's the use of going to school, anyway?" Leighton had asked Allen, his older brother, just before he left for Basic Training. "We'll just get all shot up in a war anyway."

Allen had just shrugged his shoulders, "It's something to do, Leighton."

Mrs. White, his English teacher called in Leighton's dad, "Mr. Tong, Leighton has been absent from my class too many times. Please get him to finish school."

Jack promised to encourage Leighton to attend school regularly, but he only made half-hearted attempts that didn't work. Leighton had simply lost interest in anything to do with school.

Mrs. White approached Leighton when he did come to class one day, "Look Leighton, you've missed a lot of classes, and by rights you should get an F, but I'll give you one more chance. If you turn in a good essay on this next assignment, you can still pass."

"I guess I could try."

"Leighton, you have the skills, and that's why I'm willing to give you this chance, but I'm at my very last nerve. Turn in an essay on Monday, and you will earn the credit; otherwise, you'll fail my class."

Leighton left school shortly after that, thinking. "Man I've had it. I'm already earning enough spending money and don't need this boring stuff. When I turn eighteen, I'll enlist and get ready to get shot up, too."

Marianne

1953-1954

The Western states with their wide open spaces awed the three Germans. Tilly, Leni and Marianne admired the huge Saguaro cacti in the deserts and marveled at the Southwestern architecture in the New Mexico and Arizona towns. The trip turned out to be exciting but exhausting.

"Whoa! What was that?" screamed Tilly. John's muscles tightened his grip on the steering wheel as he tried to regain control. Something had made the trailer swing back and forth. Was it going to tear loose from the car?

“I think something hit us!” John yelled as he gradually steadied the car and pulled safely onto the side of the road. His face had paled from the shock as the blood drained. Apparently a truck had tapped the back of the trailer, causing it to swerve. John was still shaking as he got out of the car to inspect the damage. He had used all his strength to keep the car under control as it lurched from side to side. Tilly, Leni and Marianne sat in stunned silence, watching the truck driver approach John.

“I see that there is a small dent back here,” the truck driver tried to down-play the damage. He almost begged John, “Would you be willing to accept $50 dollars? Please don’t call the police. I’ll get in trouble with my company, and I need this job. Look, it’s only a small scratch.”

John inspected the damage. Since no one was seriously hurt, John agreed to let the incident pass for the much-needed fifty dollars cash.

* * *

Another experience on this trip left the car damaged. In Arizona a sudden sandstorm hindered their progress. The air inside the car turned all yellow as the sand seeped through tiny openings. Outside the sand swirled mercilessly. They held cloths in front of their faces during the worst of it. When the storm was over they all got out for a breath of fresh air. “Look at this, Marianne!” yelled Tilly. Much of the paint had been stripped off the passenger side of the Packard. Marianne had had enough. She could hardly wait to get off the road and start a normal life again.

A few days later they knew that only one more hurdle had to be overcome before arriving in Victorville. “I’m not sure whether the Packard is strong enough to pull the trailer over the El Cajon

Pass. It's only a two-lane high-way, and if we get stuck on this road, we would block traffic for miles."

"What are you going to do, Dad?" Marianne, the worrier and problem-solver was curious.

"See those big tractors over there?" he pointed at a service station that was ready to help out stranded motorists. "In order to avoid trouble, we'll hire one of those to pull us up the pass."

"That's a good idea." She thought it was quite interesting to be in a car hitched to a truck and get pulled up a mountain in a caravan, but Tilly grumbled about the extra money this was going to cost.

That night the exhausted family slept soundly after finding a space in the trailer park which was to be their home for only a few weeks.

* * *

It turned out that George Air Force Base had base housing available. Tilly and John decided to put the trailer up for sale and move onto the base. Even though Marianne had enjoyed the trailer, she had to admit that it was no longer suitable for all four. The tension between Leni and Tilly and Marianne was becoming palpable. They needed some distance between them.

Leni searched the newspaper classified ads for meaningful work. Eventually she moved to Los Angeles where she worked as a housekeeper for a doctor whose wife was permanently disabled and confined to an iron lung. Tilly also found meaningful work. When Mrs. Pennington, the owner of a fabric shop in Victorville noticed that Tilly was buying a lot of fabric and Simplicity patterns, she asked, "Do you have a lot of daughters?"

"No, I only have one daughter. Why do you ask?"

"You've been buying a lot of sewing materials. Have you ever considered sewing for other people right here in our store?"

"No, I make all my daughter's clothes and my own, but I don't have many other clients. We just moved here. I did notice that you have an empty workshop back there. I'd love to have enough space to for a proper workshop."

"I'll tell you what. We'll clean up the shop and put a brand-new sewing machine back there if you will come to sew for us. You can make money for your sewing, and we will make money selling the sewing supplies. It's a good deal for both of us. What do you think?"

Tilly accepted and was pleased to be able to work in her learned trade again. John, still serving in the Air Force had his military job. Marianne had her school and friends. Finally, the family had found the peace and quiet they had yearned for.

* * *

Marianne attended Victor Valley High School. There were only a few months left of the tenth grade. She rode the school bus and became acquainted with a number of other teens from the base. She also relaxed a bit more around boys although she still wasn't interested in getting a boyfriend. Marianne became friends with Lynda Hampton and her two stepsisters who invited her to join the church choir. During summer vacation she discovered that life as a teenager was not as depressing as she had made it out to be.

The little group of teenagers included several guys. Together they went to dances at the Youth Center and joined the church choir. There was a swimming pool at the Officer's Club without a lot of young military men. “Lynda, thank you for being a friend. I’m so happy that you let me go to the swimming pool with you. I don’t like swimming in the NCO pool because of all the young military guys there.” Lynda’s dad was an officer, so the girls could spend time at the pool without being harassed. They also went to at least one movie a week and listened to music at home.

* * *

“Lynda, The Lawrence Welk Show is on TV tonight! Why don’t you come over?”

“I’ll be over after dinner.” The girls were crazy about Lawrence Welk. When they wrote notes to each other, they sealed them with the motto, "Lawrence Welk for President."

As they were watching the musical show on the 17-inch black and white TV, Lynda commented, “Wouldn’t it be nice to see these shows in color?”

“That reminds me. When I was a little girl in Germany, we had a big table model radio. Once while my grandpa was listening to Hitler making one of his loud screaming speeches, I asked him why we couldn’t see the person yelling so loud. My grandpa just looked at me and told me that the radio wasn’t big enough to put a person inside. So I told my grandpa that I wished we could be able to see stuff on the radio someday.”

“Well, I’m glad we’re seeing Lawrence Welk and not Hitler,” answered Lynda.

“Me too.”

* * *

Marianne gradually gained enough confidence around boys to let one of them actually kiss her. Exactly three weeks after her sixteenth birthday, Marianne got her first kiss!

She looked forward to her junior year, and started school with high hopes and a sense of continuity. She had already attended three different schools since her arrival in America and desperately needed to feel a sense of security. Victor Valley Union High gave her that but not for long.

When John came home with orders for Bermuda that summer, Marianne cried and cried. She didn't want to move again. She liked Victorville where she had finally become a normal American teenager, and now she was going to leave again. "I'll send for you as soon as I find a house and a school in Bermuda." Besides, there was still a lot of paperwork to be taken care of before Marianne could travel out of the country legally.

In order to reenter America after the four years in Bermuda, Marianne would need a reentry permit. The best alternative was to prove that she is already a citizen of the United States. Since her mother had already made her citizenship, Marianne was eligible, as a minor, for the derivative certificate. She had to go to a court in San Bernardino to get sworn in. "I'm so excited, Mutti! I'm actually going to be a real U.S. Citizen!" She was happy about becoming "official," but not so enthusiastic about moving on to yet another world.

Shortly after that, John took off for Bermuda, leaving Tilly and Marianne in Victorville to wait for him to arrange their move.

John wrote letters with glowing reports about Bermuda. After reading about this tropical island, Marianne started to look forward to the move; as a result, she became apathetic about attending school in Victorville anymore. When Tilly grumbled about her skipping school, she explained, "Mutti, we're going to leave in November. I just don't see the point in going to classes for two months."

"Alright, you can spend time with me in Pennington's workshop. I'll teach you about sewing clothes from store-bought patterns." Tilly's own lack of higher education made her somewhat relaxed about regular school attendance.

Secretly, Marianne promised herself not to be so stand-offish once she got to a new school. Now that she had experienced fun with friends of her own age, she was ready to become more accepting. Besides, she had read lots of advice about becoming popular in such magazines as Seventeen and True Confessions. Instead of thinking that no one wanted to be with a girl from Germany, she accepted the idea that other kids her age might be glad to have her as a friend. "*I think I can act friendly, and they will never know what a miserably shy person I have been for the past three years.*"

By late October, Marianne and her mother were ready to join John in Bermuda. Once again, both were traveling across an ocean into the unknown.

In the Museum

"What goin' on Randy? Had enough talk about wars and high school stuff?"

"Dang, yeah! All that stuff seems like old school. I have a girlfriend now. That's why I haven't been around for a couple of months."

"A girlfriend, huh? Then you'll be especially interested in the story of Leighton and Marianne. It was the Cold War that brought them together, you know?"

"How's that? We talked about the Cold War in class the other day. Apparently, it's still a popular topic in entertainment. There are a lot of post-1991 Cold War-themed feature films, novels, television, and other media . The teacher told us that movies like *Crimson Tide* (1995) are still being shown in college classes to educate students about the Cold War. I don't see what that has to do with bringing a boy and a girl together. Me 'n' my girl met in English class."

Joe shook his head but didn't correct Randy's grammar. "Yup! So do you want me to tell you more, or are you in a hurry to go see your girlfriend?"

"She's working, so I have a couple of hours to kill. Carry on, Joe."

Joe nodded, "Okay then, sit back and take notes. The Cold War affected Marianne because of her association with the United States Air Force. Skilled military men, like her stepfather, were encouraged to stay in the service. A strong military presence was required to maintain the Superpower image. The Cold War also affected Leighton. Because of the Korean War, Leighton had enlisted in the Air Force. Because of the Cold War, the Arms Race, and the Space Race, he reenlisted and became a career military man."

"I'm listening."

Leighton

1951-1953

“Hey Leighton, I heard that your brother joined the Marines.”

Leighton was just walking into the café where a small group of his buddies had gathered. “Yeah, he was listening to the radio, and they were talking about the Korean War. He drove straight over to the recruiting office so he could choose what service to join before got drafted into the army. He’s in Basic Training right now.”

“That’s nuts!” mumbled Marlowe.

“Nah! It’s just something to do,” said Tomlin.

“Just a minute guys. There’s a real shootin’ war going on over there. Somebody could get hurt,” commented Norman. “Nothing nuts about wanting to serve your country.”

The guys were enjoying some cold beer while the juke box started playing “Chattanoogie Shoe Shine Boy."

Elmer looked a little worried, “…or get killed. I’m kinda worried about my brother Ralph. He’s already over there.”

“So is mine,” said Lou.

For a moment the guys fell silent and listened to the music.

“Come on, guys. Let’s pile into my car and drive over to the bowling alley.” Leighton broke the awkward silence.

“Your car? Drive?”

“Allen gave me his old ’32 Ford when he left for Basic Training. He said I could have it.”

“Did he sign it over to you, Leighton?”

“Nah.”

“Let’s go try it out,” yelled Norman. The small group piled into the car and headed for the bowling alley.

“I can’t stay too long,” said Leighton. “I’m working at Douglas Aircraft Company in Santa Monica now. It’s dangerous work. Gotta get some sleep.” He was bragging a bit. Actually, he was just buffing pieces of sheet metal to prepare them for smooth assembly. “You guys ought to get a job. It’s kinda nice to have spending money in your pocket.”

“Hey, aren’t you in school anymore?” Norman was curious.

"No, after Allen left, I started thinking about the future. I just couldn't see it. School got boring, especially English, and so I started sleeping in instead of going to school. They called my dad in a couple of times, but that didn't help. The counselor thought I should go to Jackson where they send the truants, so I went one day. Then I quit. Forget it. I just wasn't interested."

"Man, my dad would kill me if I didn't finish high school," said Lou.

"My mom would make my life miserable if I dropped out," agreed Marlowe.

Nobody in Leighton's family had ever pushed school. He remembered how his dad enrolled him in a Saturday Chinese school a few years ago. He went a couple of times, but stopped going. Nobody had even bothered to ask him about it. Dropping out of high school was no big deal.

"Come on, let's shoot some pool before I gotta get some rest," Leighton just shrugged.

After a couple of games, the guys broke up for the night.

* * *

Leighton was looking for a job closer to home so he wouldn't have to get up so early. Lockheed was hiring, so he put in his application and gave notice at Douglas. Lockheed didn't require a high school diploma. They offered him a dollar an hour plus a 10% swing shift differential for the same work he had been doing at Douglas.

When he arrived for work one afternoon three weeks after starting at Lockheed, his supervisor called him into the office. "We notice that you have been doing good work, and you arrive on time every day. We need someone to work the 30-ton press that forms the sheet metal into the shapes needed for the hull of an airplane. Would you be interested? There's a ten-cent per hour raise involved."

Leighton asked, "Will I still be on the same shift?"

"Yes, you'll still be on the swing shift from four in the afternoon till midnight. You'll get a half hour break at eight o'clock. What do you say?"

"Sounds good sir. A dollar twenty an hour is better than a dollar ten. When do I start the new job?"

"Let's make it next Monday. See you then, son."

About two months later, Leighton was called into the section supervisor's office again. He thought, "*Now what? Am I getting fired? I thought I was doing a good job.*"

"Have a seat, son." The supervisor was smiling, so Leighton relaxed. "We need someone to procure tools and carry them to various work stations from the tool crib. It also involves some paperwork because every tool has to be accounted for. Do you think you could handle this job for us?"

"Yes sir. I'm really enjoying my work here at Lockheed."

"You'll be starting at the tool crib tomorrow. I'll train you. The guy who had this job had to leave suddenly. We need somebody in this job right away."

With thirty-six dollars take-home pay every week, Leighton enjoyed hanging out with his friends and working on his car in the small Chinatown workshop that belonged to Willie Soo Hoo. With the help of Lawrence, another friend, Leighton took the engine of his 1932 Ford Coupe apart several times.

“What do you think about making a chopped-top roadster out of this old car, Lawrence?”

“Man, that’s a lot of work with a hacksaw if you don’t have the right tools. Maybe you should leave it alone.”

“Well, I’ve got nothing better to do with my free time.”

“Time. Yeah, that’s the thing. There’s a war going on, and we’re just playing around with cars,” Lawrence had gotten thoughtful. “You know, I’ve been thinking about enlisting in the Navy.”

“Hey, good luck, Man. Once you’re in uniform you’re stuck in quite a commitment! I’m not sure whether I’m ready to commit, but the draft might get me anyway.”

Thinking about war and weapons, Lawrence suddenly remembered that Leighton had bought a rifle a couple of years before. “Hey Leighton, you still go shooting once in a while?”

Leighton looked surprised, “Shooting?”

“Yeah, don’t you have a rifle?”

“Not anymore.”

“What happened to it? Somebody steal it?”

“Nah man, you know how fifteen-year-olds are. It was only a 22 pump rifle. Gilbert and I were sitting on his front porch one day, and I was showing the gun to him. Gilbert got stupid and fired off a shot in the air. About an hour later, the police showed up and saw us sitting on the porch with the rifle.”

Lawrence asked, “You were still sitting there?”

"Yeah, we didn't think that anyone would get hurt and come looking for us."

"How did the police know it was you?"

"I guess somebody reported that a bullet struck their house. They must have figured out what direction it was coming from. They drove around till they noticed us sitting there with that stupid gun."

"Did you get arrested?"

"No, they just took the gun away and told me that I could reclaim it when I turned twenty-one."

Lawrence got thoughtful. "Funny, here we are only eighteen and the country is ready to draft us into a real shooting war. They ought to at least give you your rifle back now."

* * *

A few days later, the Sino-Mercs gathered at the café again. "Man, I've been thinking about Korea all week," said Elmer. "I've got half a mind to walk right over to the recruiting office."

"Funny! Even at Lockheed, where they're building more and more airplanes, I've been thinking the same thing," said Leighton.

"What do you hear from Allen?" Benny wanted to know. "Is he in the shooting war?"

"No, actually he's kind of lucky. They tested him and found out that he has English and typing skills, so they trained him as a stenographer. He's working in a regular building, maybe even headquarters. He's in communications."

"Lucky!"

"Hey, I just got an idea," said Norman. "Let's drive over to the recruiting station and join the Air Force. That way we won't get drafted into the Army."

"You're nuts!" laughed Benny.

Stanley said, "They won't take me with my crippled leg."

"You're plenty smart to get a good job right here, Stanley. Not everybody needs to be in uniform to serve their country," Leighton tried to keep the conversation light. "Anyway, Norman, I don't think your idea is nuts at all. I hear that the Air Force needs a lot of good men. It looks like the Russians are building up their military."

"Yeah, for some reason, the superpowers were Allies in World War II, and now they are fighting against each other in Korea. It's a crazy world. A war like that could spread and start another world war," added Tomlin.

"What a mess! Here we are, a bunch of kids who are supposed to fight in wars to keep peace in the world, and some of us didn't even finish high school. I think we're in for a hell of a ride!" mumbled Elmer.

"Well? Who's in? Recruiting station at nine tomorrow morning?" demanded Norman.

Eight hands shot up. "The Sino-Mercs will take care of the world!" Leighton and Norman laughed, but they were dead serious. "Ok. There's ten of us. Let's do it!"

* * *

The recruiting sergeant looked at the ten Chinese guys walking into the office. "What's happenin'? Can I help you?"

Leighton spoke up, "We're here to enlist."

"Come on, guys! Is this a joke?"

"No joke, Man. Some of us already have brothers over there."

"Over there?"

"Yeah, in Korea. We wanna enlist."

The recruiting sergeant was convinced they weren't joking. "Let me get the forms. You can fill them out over there on that table."

All ten guys were accepted and left within a week of each other. In October 1952, Leighton, Norman, Sammy, Alfred, Tomlin and the others joined the Air Force.

* * *

"Are they sending you to Parks too, Norman?"

"I guess Sammy, you and I are going to Parks AFB for Basic Training on a bus tomorrow afternoon if we pass our physicals today. Man, I don't like standing in line to get these shots."

Leighton said, "They're just trying to make sure we're healthy and all caught up with our vaccinations. A few shots now to prevent more trouble later. That's okay with me."

"I suppose so," nodded Norman. "Okay, see you at the bus stop after lunch tomorrow."

* * *

Arriving at Parks at three in the morning, the boys were taken to a barracks. They quickly fell asleep on the cots with bare mattresses. At seven they were roused for a march to breakfast. Afterwards, they joined a large number of new recruits like themselves in a march to a huge warehouse.

A tall tough-looking sergeant bellowed, "Recruits! You will form lines and wait your turn. You will remain silent and accept your bedding and other items. When a uniformed person addresses you, you will respond with 'Yes Sir.' Is that clear?"

A loud resounding "Yes Sir," echoed through the large hall.

Leighton waited anxiously in line for his uniform. He was issued a dress uniform that included a brimmed hat, a utility uniform that included two caps, shoes and socks, underwear, and his personalized dog tags. In another line he received the bedding and a duffel bag for the uniform items.

Back in the barracks, Leighton was assigned a cot, a footlocker and a space to hang his uniform. The open bay accommodated around forty new recruits. Two sergeants, called TI's (training instructors) with loud whistles were continually on duty to supervise the recruits and issue orders for all activities.

Training began promptly at six the next morning. The boys were roused to stand next to their cots. A TI announced, "Each morning you are to wash up and get dressed in your utility uniform, march in formation to breakfast, return to straighten your bunks. Today after breakfast, you will stamp your last name initial and the last four of your SSN on your underwear and uniform. You will be taught how to fold and position each item in your footlocker. Talking amongst yourselves is permitted while at ease, but silence is to be maintained while you are in formation, either standing or marching. Now you have thirty minutes to take care of personal business and get dressed in your utility uniform. When the whistle blows you are to step outside as quickly as possible and stand for your first inspection. You will form a straight line and wait silently for further instructions. Is that clear?"

"Yes Sir!" mumbled several voices.

"Let's try that again, and this time everyone in unison."

"Yes Sir!" loud and clear.

It didn't take long for the recruits to get accustomed to the routine of marching in formation to every activity, including the classes on Military Justice, History and various Ceremonies.

* * *

"Hey, Norman, did you earn a pass, too? Sammy and I already got ours," asked Leighton.

"Yeah! It's a good thing. I was starting to go crazy from all this military routine."

"Well, they warned us that we would have to stay and participate for six weeks before earning our first thirty-six hour weekend pass."

Several of the original Sino-Mercs were stationed at Parks for their Basic Training, so they planned to spend their weekend passes together. They took the bus to San Francisco, rented a room and enjoyed some time at the Jade Palace, a cozy lounge in Chinatown. For New Year's Eve that year, the gang was invited to a party by Alfred's uncle Ernie.

"What are you wearing to the party, Alfred?" asked Leighton.

"I only have the same clothes we arrived in."

"Me too. I forgot that we'd get passes to go to parties."

"Everybody is just wearing casual clothes. My uncle won't care."

* * *

Arriving at the party, Leighton was surprised to see almost three hundred people in a huge hall. It seemed like all the girls were escorted by their boyfriends. The Sino-Mercs realized they probably wouldn't have any chances to dance.

"Let's wait till midnight, and then walk around kissing as many girls as possible!" suggested Norman.

"Good idea. I hope I'm not too drunk by then," laughed Sammy.

"I'm staying sober for the chance to kiss the girls," declared Leighton.

Promptly at midnight, the kissing started, but it lasted only for a few minutes before the boyfriends demanded their girls back.

"Whooo Hooo! That was fun!" yelled Alfred just as a big guy walked over to claim his girl. "Alright, alright, Man. It's New Year's Eve, and I didn't mean anything by stealing a little kiss."

The big guy stared at him.

Alfred's uncle came over, "Let's not start anything. It's been a good party, and now you boys need to get some rest before going back to Parks."

The big guy smirked, "Oh you guys are new recruits at Parks?"

"Yeah."

"I'll let you get off this time, but if you ever mess with my girl again, you'll get a war right here in Chinatown."

"Yes Sir!" Alfred, Norman and Leighton mock-saluted, and then left.

They walked the three blocks in the cool night air back to the hotel. "Holy crap! How did all these people know about our room? Did the Sino-Mercs bring 'em along?"

About fifteen other recruits from Parks had managed to get into the room. They were on the floor, the couch, the bed, and one was even lying next to the bathtub. "I was hoping to sleep in a nice comfortable bed, and now I'll be glad to find a spot on the floor. Oh well, G'night, fellas," whispered Leighton as he squeezed between two snoring strangers.

* * *

Once Basic Training at Parks AFB was finished, Leighton, Norman and Sammy were transferred to Keesler Air Force Base in Mississippi for training in their specific jobs. Leighton's training in Basic Electronics was to last for twenty-two weeks, and his training in Electronic Countermeasures Equipment Maintenance (ECM) was to last for an additional twelve weeks. Norman and Sammy were training at the Radio Operators School, also at Keesler.

The boys had more freedom after classes and on weekends than they had at Parks. With their passes, they took weekend trips into New Orleans. They found several local Chinese businesses by looking in the telephone book.

"Hello?"

Leighton held the telephone close, "I'm Chinese. A bunch of us from Los Angeles is stationed here at Keesler, and we wondered whether there was anything going on in the New Orleans Chinese community."

"You're in the Air Force?" the voice wanted to know.

"Yes Sir!" Leighton responded automatically, and then he thought, "*Man this training is really working*."

"What kind of community are you looking for?" the voice asked.

"Oh, we get weekend passes and just want to get away for a few hours to be with Chinese people. We like bowling or playing pool."

"Well, we have a Chinese bowling league. We meet on Friday nights at the Mid-City Lanes Rock 'n Bowl. If you come by, we can introduce each other."

"Thanks."

After classes on Friday, Leighton and the boys caught a bus to New Orleans. The Chinese bowlers welcomed them and invited them to make themselves comfortable behind the settee area. For a couple of hours they relaxed with some drinks while watching the teams bowl.

"Hey boys," said the guy with the familiar phone voice. "We're having a dance party next weekend. Let me write down the address, and here are some more phone numbers of Chinese businesses around town. We're all friends. You're welcome to join us."

Sammy and Norman smiled. “That would be great. We’ll be there.”

Leighton said, “We really appreciate your hospitality. We didn’t know how to act in the South. We had heard some strange things about Mississippi, but we figured a big city like New Orleans would be okay.”

“Yes, boys, there is still a lot of old-fashioned racism going on around here. Just follow the rules and stay out of trouble. You’ll be alright.”

The boys made lots of visits to New Orleans to bowl, dance and even swim with their new-found friends.

* * *

In September 1953, Leighton was assigned to Kelly Air Force Base in San Antonio, Texas. His job was to remove and replace the radio and radar equipment on C-54 aircraft. He was surprised that this task had nothing to do with his training in ECM, but soon rationalized, “Oh well, electronics is electronics.”

Leighton spent some of his free time in San Antonio where he met a Chinese girl named Frances. Apparently, the “voice” in New Orleans had informed the Chinese community in San Antonio that one of the Chinese guys stationed at Keesler was coming to Kelly Air Force Base. “Make that Chinese boy from Los Angeles feel welcome.” Leighton got to know several people and had a good time in Texas.

Frances invited Leighton to a special New Year’s event. “Hey, a group of us from San Antonio is driving up to Houston for a big New Year’s Eve party. I’d love for you to come with us.”

"I was planning to hang out with my brother Gene who is stationed at Lackland."

"You have a brother at Lackland?"

"Yeah, he just got there. Seeing that Lackland is right next to Kelly, we've been visiting. We didn't grow up together, so it's been great getting to know each other better."

"Well, he can come too. The more the merrier, I always say," laughed Frances.

"You sure?"

"Sure. If your brother is half as nice as you, we'll get along just fine."

* * *

One day in January, Leighton received orders for his new assignment. He was nervous as he opened the envelope. "*Am I going to Korea?*" he wondered.

"Bermuda!" he read it out loud two times just to be sure. "Bermuda! I didn't even know we had an Air Force Base there."

When he told the other guys in the shop about his orders, they all offered to trade their assignments with him. "I think I'm willing to sacrifice and serve my country in Bermuda," he smiled as he declined their generous offers.

Gene was happy for him. "You ought to go home before you go to Bermuda. Did you know that Mom got released from the hospital?"

"What? I heard that Mom's cousin Edward Vann was visiting, but I didn't hear anything about Mom being home. What happened? Tell me everything you know, Gene."

Gene began to explain. "Let's go have a beer. It's a long and complicated story."

"Well, you've got me all curious now. I've been gone from home for nearly two years," said Leighton.

"When you left in 1952, Dad asked me and Jerry to move in with him. I guess the house got a little too empty for him. Well, it filled up pretty quick. Uncle George and his wife moved in with us a couple of months later."

"I thought Uncle George was working in Oakland with Ted."

"He was, but he wasn't happy there. He kept asking Dad to help him get a job in Los Angeles, so finally Dad said for him to come and that there were plenty of jobs in the area. George found a job in a grocery store right away, so he brought his wife, and they moved into our house on Cleveland Street."

"That wreck?"

"Yeah, and it hasn't gotten any better. Anyway, at least it's big enough. Uncle George and Ng Yow Wan moved into the back bedroom. Jerry and I slept in the same room next to Dad's, and that was quite an adventure with his snoring."

"Oh yeah, I remember that snoring after he had a couple of swigs from the bottle of Scotch he always kept around. Sometimes the whole house rattled."

Gene agreed, "And! He still smokes those strong cigarettes and has a couple of swigs before he goes to bed."

"You said Mom was home now. How did that happen?"

Gene continued, "Well, you remember her cousin Edward Vann."

"Is he the one who is half black and grew up in Augusta?"

"That's the one. He joined the Air Force during World War II and became a pilot. He was one of the volunteer pilots that went over to China and helped the Chinese Air Force defend themselves against the Japanese who were invading China. After the war, he brought back a wife and a couple of kids."

"A wife and kids?"

"Yes, his Chinese copilot made him promise to take care of his wife and two little daughters in case he got killed. Well, the Chinese colonel did get killed. So when Edward Vann went to visit his widow, he fell in love and married her. He took his new family to Augusta, Georgia where he grew up."

"The guy's a real hero. Did you say he was Mom's cousin?"

"Yes, he is. Edward's father and Mom's father are brothers. There were four sons in that family. Our grandfather came to America in 1879 and established the Herbal shop in San Francisco. A few years later, Edward Vann's father also immigrated and moved to Augusta, Georgia."

"Why to Augusta?"

"The city wanted to build some kind of canal, and there weren't enough local laborers. So the city hired a lot of the Chinese laborers who weren't needed on the railroad anymore. They were brought in to help build that canal in Augusta."

"The same Chinese that built the railroad during the Gold Rush?"

"Yeah maybe the same ones. I don't know that for sure. Laborers like that aren't allowed to bring their wives over here, and they have to go back to China when their contract is up. Anyway, the Chinese laborers who were building the canal in Augusta needed to have a place to shop for food, so the city allowed a few Chinese merchants and other businesses to form a small Chinatown. When our grandfather's brother Wong Kam Chen immigrated, he decided to move to Augusta and open a grocery store. Later he even owned a laundry business. He fell in love with a black girl, but he wasn't allowed to marry her. They lived together and had three children. Edward Vann was the oldest."

"I know about those laws. Between the miscegenation laws, the Chinese Exclusion laws, and the Jim Crow laws, a young person in this country could go crazy!" Leighton remembered being told to move from one seat on a bus to another one.

Gene agreed, "But at least in Los Angeles, we didn't really feel all that craziness."

"In our grandfather's time only merchants and some teachers were allowed privileges," said Leighton. "But how does all this have anything to do with Mom?"

"Okay, after Edward Vann and his family got all settled down in Augusta, he decided to take a vacation to California and visit all the cousins he hadn't seen in a long time and meet some he had never met before. When he found out that Mom had been in a mental hospital he went to visit her…"

"…and he noticed that she wasn't crazy at all. Right?" interrupted Leighton.

"Right. He had a long talk with Dad and Uncle George. The three of them decided to bring Mom home. George's wife would be there to help with Mom if she needed anything during the day while Uncle George and Dad were at work, and Jerry was at school."

"Sounds like a good plan. Man! My mind is reeling from all this new information. You've got me convinced. I'll request a leave to go home before I go to Bermuda. I hope Mom remembers me. She hasn't really seen me very often as an adult."

"She's good, Leighton. You'd be surprised how well she's doing."

"I'll take a leave in May, and then I have to report to Kindley Air Force Base in Bermuda on the first of June. Thanks for the beer and the info, Gene."

"My pleasure. See you this weekend."

Marianne

1954-1955

"*God, I hate this typing stuff!*" The small classroom was clattering with Underwoods, Royals and Smith Coronas. Marianne whispered to Lillian who was making eyes at Denis again. "Are we decorating tonight?" Several of the girls nodded. Sternly, Sister Katherine warned them to keep typing or there wouldn't be a dance.

"My Papier-Mache snowman is finished," Marianne told Lillian as the students were pouring from the school.

"Are you sure that Denis can get his dad's car to carry it to school?"

"Yes, it'll be big enough, and he lets him drive it whenever he wants."

The theme for the Junior-Senior dance was Winter Wonderland. It had been Marianne's idea. She still couldn't believe that she had become so popular. Her theory had worked. Suddenly her thoughts drifted back to the first day at Mount Saint Agnes.

"Once my mom, dad and I had gotten settled into the typical Bermudian house on Serpentine Road, making arrangements for school was next. Kindley Air Force Base had no school facilities for high school age dependents, so they enrolled me in Mount Saint Agnes, a Catholic high school taught by the Sisters of Charity.

I was pleased that MSA was within walking distance of our home in Hamilton, but my old reluctance to make new friends threatened to assert itself on the first day during lunch break. "They don't want me." I almost avoided the group of girls laughing and carrying on near the door of the lunch room, but she thought, "No, by golly, I promised myself. No negative thoughts!"

"Hi, my name is Marianne." Friendly smile on face. Fear of rejection inside.

"Hi, I'm Rosalie and here are Jacqueline, Barbara, Nora and Jennifer. Where are you from?"

They had noticed my German accent already; I started to withdraw. Mentally, I slapped my own face. "NO! I'm not going to fall for it," so I simply said, "I'm from Germany."

"Wow, that's groovy. How did you get to Bermuda?" They were actually interested. Nice girls.

Lillian yelled, "Come on, Marianne, stop thinking so much. We have work to do."

"Sorry, I'm back. Ha ha, I just took a little time-warp trip."

Lillian and a couple of other girls laughed.

* * *

In time, the sixteen eleventh-grade girls had shared their stories and studies. The junior class consisted of only seventeen students. Octave Coelho was the one boy. Sister Vincent, the strict nun, was the English and history teacher. Sister Elizabeth, the funny one, taught Science and Math. Sister Katherine taught Religion, Shorthand and Typing. How Marianne hated that typing! Memories of the ninth-grade torture chamber in Cedar Rapids often overwhelmed her, but she persevered. All the eleventh graders were attempting to qualify for the Cambridge Oversea School Certificate. This was a big deal because the certificate would qualify the holder to enter Cambridge University. Only eight of the sixteen, including Marianne, qualified to take the exam. Marianne got so stressed out over a science experiment and all the other strict requirements that she ended up in the hospital for two weeks with pneumonia.

She gratefully received the visits of Sister Elizabeth and Sister Katherine who brought her a tiny charm on a neck chain. Another week of convalescence with her mother's home cooking, and Marianne was ready to continue her studies. That junior year had been a tough one for her.

* * *

Now the exams were behind them, and the girls were decorating for the Spring Dance called Winter Wonderland.

“Are you bringing Bill to the dance?” Rosalie wondered.

“Yes, we're still going steady,” Marianne hesitated a little. Not having an education beyond the eighth grade, Bill was somehow beneath Mount Saint Agnes students. Some of the girls openly snubbed him.

“It's okay. Don't feel bad. If you like him, that's all that matters.”

“I know.” In the hubbub of decorating the hall any doubts left her. Her home-made Papier-Mache snowman had a prominent place on the stage and ivory soap snow was piled up in each small window pane. It had never snowed in Bermuda, so everyone was quite excited about the theme.

Marianne and Bill had a great time at the dance.

* * *

Usually their dates were more boring. They walked to the movies. He didn’t have enough money for anything else. Even though there were many great beaches in Bermuda, Bill seldom took advantage of them. Movies, movies, movies. Bill was okay as a boyfriend, but Marianne knew that he would never become her husband. He had no job; as a result, he had no money to spend on entertainment or transportation. Even at his age of twenty-one, he was still asking his mother for movie money. Marianne suspected that he wouldn’t have had any imagination for more exciting dates even if he had enough money. Marianne was going out with him because he was good-looking and lived next door. There weren’t any other boys her age in her neighborhood.

* * *

She was growing up. A senior in high school. Despite all the fun, thoughts about her future sobered her. There was no money for college even though she had earned the Cambridge Oversea School Certificate. “Do you think we’re rich? We can’t afford to send you to college,” her stepfather responded when Marianne brought up her desire to study Electronics at a University. “Learn something feminine and make a husband happy!”

Oh well, Marianne wasn't sure she was ready to leave home, anyhow. She had found a comfort zone and didn’t want it to end yet. Another move to somewhere in the world was not a pleasant thought. Staying with her parents was the more comfortable alternative. She was looking forward to graduation with mixed emotions.

“You mean we won't wear caps and gowns?” Marianne was a little disappointed when Rosalie mentioned what MSA students wear at graduation.

“No, it's a tradition for Mount Saint Agnes girls to wear white formals for graduation. It's beautiful.” Rosalie explained.

* * *

“Mutti, you have to make me a white formal!”

"What? Why? Are you getting married?” Tilly looked up from her sewing machine in surprise.

“No. They wear white formals for graduation here. Jacqueline Soose wants to know whether you can make her one too,” Marianne blurted out.

Tilly made two beautiful gowns. Graduation was a hit.

* * *

Tilly approached Marianne a couple of weeks after graduation. “Don’t you think it’s time for you to find a job?”

“Mutti, how am I going to find a job here in Bermuda?”

“Have you applied on the base yet?”

“On the base? I don’t want to join the Air Force.”

John joined the conversation, “Marianne, there are lots of civilians working on the base. In the Base Exchange, for example. Support services, such as the BX, the bowling alley, and lots of other services the civilian employees are paid out of Non-appropriated funds, while the Air Force itself is funded by Appropriated Funds. Civilians can work in the support services. Do you want me to bring you an application?”

“That would be great, Daddy.”

Tilly agreed, “If Marianne can get a job in the BX, she’ll think more of herself as an adult than just a school girl.”

Marianne really was just a school girl. She was hesitant about joining the world of adults. Her confidence in herself had been tested so often that she didn’t appreciate just how much she had already accomplished.

“Do you really believe I could go to work?”

“Sure, why not?”

* * *

Flo Black, the manager of the Terminal Branch of the Main Exchange, interviewed Marianne. “We have an opening at the stationery counter. That job also includes dealing with the daily deliveries of three New York newspapers and working the cash register. Do you think you could handle that?"

"I was very good in Math, so I know I could handle the cash register. Please tell me about those newspapers."

Flo explained, "The three o'clock plane from New York brings about a hundred copies of newspapers every day. There are four types, The New York Times, The Daily News, The Journal-American and The Herald-Tribune. Somebody then brings the bundles to us here at the Terminal. We have to count them and put them out for sale at the stationery counter."

"Oh, that would be part of my job?"

"Yes, but there's another part. Before putting them on the counter, you would have to come to the stock room in back check the subscriptions."

"Subscriptions?"

"There are some people who pay a month in advance for their newspapers. That's what we call a subscription. You'll have to collect the money and keep a ledger. You also have to make sure that enough papers are set aside for the subscribers, so when they come in, their papers are waiting for them. Some people only come in once a week, so you'll have to save their papers for them. The rest of the newspapers are for sale to anyone who wants them. Being this is the main airport in the Atlantic Ocean, we have lots of travelers who stop by this little Terminal BX. You'll have to be friendly and efficient. What do you say?"

Marianne was smiling. “This sounds like a wonderful job. I’d love to work here, and I think I’ll be able to take care of the newspapers and all the other things on the stationery counter.”

“Alright, young lady. You can come in tomorrow and I’ll show you around. Oh, by the way, the hours are nine to six with an hour from twelve to one for lunch. The pay is 80 cents an hour for eight hours a day.”

“Thank you, Mrs. Black. Do you want me to come in at nine?”

“Yes, at nine. We will have an hour before the doors open to the public. That should be enough time to get situated. Our store hours are from ten to six.”

“Alright, Good bye, and thank you again.”

Marianne rode home on her motorized bicycle called a Moped and yelled into the house, “Mutti, I got the job!”

In the Library

"Hey Joe, how's it going?"

"I'm getting the hang of this fancy phone of mine. I have a couple of game apps, and guess what!"

"What?"

"I've been texting my grown kids and grandkids. They've been wanting me to get one of these gadgets because they all have these smartphones. They never had time to spend talking on the phone, but now with texting we can stay in touch. It's like magic!"

"I'm glad I was able to help, Joe. Guess what's been going on with me!"

"What?"

"I've been telling my girlfriend about those two kids, Marianne and Leighton, and now she wants me to find out the important ending."

"Okay. I'll tell you about Leighton and then I'll have to tell you about another war."

"No, no more wars, no more wars!" Randy started waving his notebook like a protester's poster.

"It's not the kind of war you're protesting, Randy. It's the war that Marianne and Leighton had to fight against the world. Do you remember the word miscegenation?"

"Yeah, so what?"

"Sit down, relax and I'll tell you."

Leighton

1954-1955

Bermuda turned out to be a dream assignment. Even the barracks were a friendly place to find new friends.

"Hey, Dave. I'll be gone for the whole month of June. I'm going to take a leave and visit my folks."

"The Air Force will go on without you, but what about your job at the BX?"

Leighton was sure that Flo, the manager, could manage without him. He had been the night supervisor at the small terminal branch of the Base Exchange, but there were plenty of other employees who could step in.

"If I lose that job, I lose it. It's not a big deal."

With private transportation being quite costly, Leighton decided to try his luck with the military "Space Available" flights.

“Sorry, son, we only have flights going to Mcguire Air Force Base from here. At Mcguire, you’ll probably be able to catch a hop to Charleston,” the scheduler at the terminal told Leighton.

“That’s fine as long as I get to Los Angeles eventually.”

In Charleston, Leighton caught a flight to San Antonio, Texas. There were some friends he wanted to visit.

Frances was happy to see him again, “Tell me about Bermuda.”

“It’s amazing. I’ve even bought some golf clubs and learned to play golf. It rains sometimes, but it clears up quickly. The weather is great the year around. For transportation, I have a motorcycle. The maximum speed limit on all Bermuda roads is twenty miles per hour, so there are very few accidents.”

“So why are you already leaving Bermuda?”

“It’s been a year since I’ve seen my folks, so I thought I’d take some vacation time to visit the mainland. I especially wanted to see you again.”

Frances smiled. “Good thinking. Do you have a place to stay while you’re in San Antonio?”

“Yes, I’m staying in the transit quarters on Kelly Air Force Base.”

“Come over for dinner tonight.”

“Thanks, we’ll take in a movie afterwards. Now I’ll have to see about getting a flight to California. See you around five, OK?”

There was only one flight leaving for California that week, so Leighton spent a couple more days with Frances before leaving for Riverside.

* * *

In Riverside, he had to catch a bus to Los Angeles. Many of his friends were still in the military, but Stanley was happy to see him. "Lookin' good, Leighton! The Air Force must be treating you right."

"Thanks. How's life treating you, Stanley?"

"Well, you know. Been working a bit in my folk's store to earn enough money for my habit."

"Habit? Oh yeah! Still smoking marijuana, huh?" remembered Leighton.

"Sure, got nothin' better to do around here."

Leighton suggested, "Let's go to Man Jin Lo after dinner. I'm going home right now to see my mother for a while. Later I'll have time to visit with you some more."

Stanley said, "Ok see you later."

Leighton's mother was happy to see him, but there was very little conversation. She had completely given up speaking English. Perhaps it reminded her too much of the years in the English-speaking hospital. Leighton had never really learned to speak adult Chinese. He only remembered the language of his childhood; however, he felt at home with his family and spent as much time during the day as possible with them. In the evenings, he went out to find his friends.

Man Jin Lo was a favorite hang-out in New Chinatown. The place had a sunken piano bar where Herbie played every night. "Has Stanley showed up yet?" asked Leighton as the waitress brought him a beer.

"Not yet, but I'm sure he'll be here soon."

A pretty girl and Stanley bumped into each other as they both walked through the door. "Sorry, sometimes I'm a little off balance," explained Stanley.

The girl smiled, "Don't worry, I'm not that breakable."

Leighton got up and invited the girl to take a seat. "We're just hanging out and listening to Herbie play the piano. Come sit with us."

She accepted the invitation, "My name is Barbara, and I'm just passing through."

"Passing through? From where to where?"

"Well, I'm from Hawaii, and I studied in Kalamazoo, Michigan for a year. Right now I'm in Los Angeles to do some sight-seeing before I go back to Hawaii. I'm staying with friends in Pasadena."

"Sounds like a nice trip. Have you seen Hollywood yet?"

"Yes, I took a bus tour all over the area yesterday. I even took a picture of the Hollywood sign on the mountain."

The boys spent a very pleasant evening in the unexpected company of a pretty girl.

Leighton said, "Too bad we're both leaving soon. I would love to get to know you better."

Stanley commented, "People are always leaving me behind. Dang it! Sometimes I just want to get out of here, but I never have enough money."

Leighton and Barbara had no answer for him. "Wow, listen to that beautiful song Herbie is playing. 'What Kind of Fool Am I' is just the right song for the mood we're in."

"Let's just enjoy the moment," suggested Barbara. She glanced at her watch. "Uh oh, I think I missed the last bus back to Pasadena."

"Hey, I've got my car. We'll take you back to your friends' house," said Stanley.

In the backseat, Leighton and Barbara necked all the way to Pasadena. Barbara whispered, "Dang, I can't believe that we both have to go back to islands in two different oceans. Bermuda and Hawaii are a whole world apart. I'd sure like to get to know you better."

Leighton got philosophical, "Life is very strange. People travel all over the world. We meet people, but we can't stay with them. Too many other obligations. If it's meant to be, perhaps we'll meet again."

Stanley interrupted the passion in the back seat, "Hey guys, we're here. This is the address you gave me. Time to stop the Roman hands and Russian fingers."

Barbara waved a friendly 'Good-bye" as she quickly slipped into the house.

* * *

"Time to go back," Leighton told his family. "I'll see you next year."

There were no military "Space Available" flights out of Los Angeles, so Leighton decided to pay for his way back. Arriving at La Guardia, he discovered that the next flight to Bermuda was two hours later. He settled into a comfortable seat in the terminal and promptly fell asleep. He awoke just in time to realize that the plane to Bermuda had left already.

"*Man, the next PanAm flight to Bermuda is not till tomorrow! What the heck am I going to do now?*" He noticed a poster for bus rides to Manhattan. "*Maybe I should do some sight-seeing while I'm here.*"

After roaming around Broadway and 42nd Street for a few hours, Leighton took the bus back to LaGuardia where he spent an uncomfortable night in the terminal.

* * *

Back in the barracks, his cot welcomed him, and he slept for eight solid hours.

Dave roused him. "Hey man, you look exhausted. You must have had a wild vacation."

"It was okay, but I missed my flight and ended up spending the night in the terminal at La Guardia. I'm glad I'm back.

"I'm sure Flo will be glad you're back, too. She asked me several times if I wanted your old job, and I told her no. My Air Force job is just enough work for me. "

Leighton said, "I like the extra money. I'll let her know I'm back after I check back in with my First Sergeant."

The Romance War

1955-1956

"Oh Hi, Tom! It's great to have you back!" Flo's voice caught Marianne's attention as she was sorting the subscriptions to the newspapers brought in daily from New York. She looked up, and a wave of warmth swept over her. There stood God--tall, dark and fantastic--talking to Flo, the manager of the Terminal branch of the Kindley Air Base Exchange. Though their eyes didn't meet, her heart began to stir. She quickly bent down to concentrate on her work.

Marianne had accepted a job at the stationery counter in the small BX branch which carried items a traveler might want to pick up between trips. Her work in the terminal BX had become a comfortable routine. Graduation from high school was just behind, and now her duties included counting out the daily newspaper subscription, putting the leftovers out for sale, and trashing the out-of-date ones. She also had to keep her station neat and display attractive merchandise, such as Parker pen and pencil sets and boxes of decorative stationery in the glass case which served as the counter. The important thing was to make sure that the money in her register matched the receipts. She loved her eighty cents an hour job. She was now officially grown up!

* * *

"Hi!" Coal-black Asian eyes, beautiful teeth and a disarming smile approached Marianne's counter carrying an armful of newspapers.

"*Oh, my God, here he comes!*" she thought as "Tom" put the newspapers on the counter. He had already counted them.

"The airplane from New York was a bit early today, so I thought I'd bring the newspapers to you." His voice was heavenly.

"*So he's not only good-looking but also helpful*!" She thought as she felt the same unfamiliar but pleasant feeling she had felt when she noticed him the day before. Warmth. Maybe it was just Bermuda's July heat washing over her.

"Thanks for doing those newspapers for me. I was just getting ready to go in the backroom to count them." She tried to be as nonchalant as her eighteen-year-old heart could manage. "You didn't have to do that."

"It's alright. I'm working here part-time again. I used to work here, but I went back to the States for a month."

"Are you a dependent, too?" She wondered out loud while all kinds of ideas chased each other through her mind.

"No, I'm in the Air Force, in 'Com/Nav.' I work here in the BX for extra money to send home to my folks. I'll be around. Bye."

Another thought flew by, "*So he's generous, too. And he cares about his family.*"

Then he was gone. Marianne busied herself with the newspapers and soon forgot the gorgeous smile that had walked into her life. Her stepfather came by after five to pick her up after work. Since she didn't get off till six, John bought a newspaper and waited for her in the cafeteria. On the way home, she remembered the smile and dreamily wondered how she could get to know "Tom" better. A plan was forming.

Life was good. Bermuda's great climate, high school graduation, her mother's happiness, her own room, a boy friend named Bill, and an exciting job was all Marianne needed to make her believe she had landed in Paradise. Things were about to change.

"Gosh, I didn't expect you to do my newspapers again!"

"It's my pleasure." A quick smile, and he was gone.

Actually, it was Marianne's pleasure. She hadn't been dreaming; he was real. Gradually, Bill's image was being replaced by Tom's.

Just before she got off work a few days later, he suddenly stood in front of her counter again. "I thought I'd buy one of those newspapers."

Tom was in uniform. His name tag read "Tong."

"I thought your name was Tom. Isn't that what Flo Black, the manager, called you the other day?"

"Flo calls me by my last name. My full name is Leighton Hall Lai Tong."

"What nationality is that?"

"Chinese."

"I've never met a Chinese before. I always thought that Chinese people are very small. You're so tall. I thought you were Hawaiian. How tall are you?" Marianne's blabbering mouth proved she was obviously a silly eighteen. She couldn't stop the gibberish. Blather, blather, bla...

"I'm six feet tall. I think my ancestors were mountain people."

"Like Genghis Khan? That's great. I think I have Attila the Hun in my background!" They both laughed.

"You look cute with that little black nose." His finger gently wiped away a smudge of newsprint. "See you tomorrow."

It was a little more difficult to forget the smile this time despite a number of other customers crowding the cash register.

Her imagination reeled. "*What should I call him? His name isn't Tom. Should I call him Leighton? That's a beautiful name, but I've already gotten used to thinking about him as Tom. Oh, never mind. Bill is waiting to take me to a movie, and I really have no business dreaming about a Chinese guy no matter what his name is.*" Even if he was the most handsome, generous, considerate, and graceful creature Marianne had ever met.

* * *

One of the most exciting holidays in Bermuda is the annual Festival of the August Moon. The two days of festivities which included a parade of boat floats on the Hamilton Harbor and lots of fun in the streets, were about to help Marianne take control of her fate.

When Tong appeared at the newspaper counter with his friend Dave, Marianne asked, "Have you ever gone to the Festival of the August Moon in Hamilton?" They hadn't.

“Oh, you should go. There is going to be all kinds of fun this weekend,” she oozed. “My boyfriend Bill is taking me.”

“Well, if we both can get the night off from work, it might be nice to see what it's all about.” Dave agreed.

“How will you get there?” she asked, smiling at Tong.

“Dave and I both have motorcycles. Transportation is no problem. We’ll probably just take Dave’s bike. It’s big enough for both of us. I’ll have to drive because he doesn’t have his Bermuda license yet.”

“He has a motorcycle but no license?”

“Dave has a license to drive on base, but he’s not old enough to get a license to drive on Bermudian roads.”

“Oh.” Marianne melted at the sound of his calm explanation.

* * *

Back at the barracks, Dave and Leighton talked about Marianne for a while. “She’s real pretty,” said Dave casually.

“I think she’s beautiful, and her smile makes me feel all funny inside,” declared Leighton.

“Who’s beautiful and makes you feel funny?” Triplett, Leighton’s roommate had just walked in on the conversation.

Dave explained, “He’s met this new girl at the newspaper counter in the Terminal, and now he can hardly remember his own name.”

Triplett laughed. “Yeah, I’ve seen her. She’s real pretty. Have you taken her out yet, Leighton?”

"No. I don't think she'd go out with me. I know her dad. He works in Engine Build-up. He's a big guy and not very friendly to me."

"He doesn't seem like a prejudiced guy," said Dave.

"Maybe not to you, but I get a weird feeling whenever he comes over and talks to me in the Com/Nav (Communications-Navigation) shop. Dating his daughter might open up more trouble than I want to deal with," answered Leighton.

"Just play it cool. We'll go out together one of these days, and then you can see whether she's interested," offered Dave.

* * *

Marianne was smug. The seed had been planted. The guys would probably come to Hamilton for the Festival of the August Moon. Now all she had figure out is how to get to Hamilton without Bill. This would not be easy. Her parents would not let her go out alone at night. (Apparently, they had forgotten that she had traveled without a chaperone for two weeks from Germany to America when she was only thirteen.)

On Saturday evening Marianne suddenly developed a "headache." She sent Bill away, "Sorry, Honey, I'm going to stay home and go to bed early. See you tomorrow."

She moped around the house for a while. Tilly was worried, "What's wrong? I thought you were going to the Festival."

"Bill isn't feeling well, so we called off our date."

Tilly sympathized, "You know, the Glidewell's will be going. Maybe you can go with them." The Glidewell's were a young American couple who lived downstairs. "Why don't you ask whether you can go with them?"

"That's a great idea, Mutti, but I don't have enough money."

"Here's a couple of dollars. Have a good time, but don't get lost in the crowd. With so many strange people, you never know what could happen." If she only knew what Marianne had dreamed up!

The Glidewell's and Marianne walked the two miles to downtown Hamilton. The town was aglitter with excitement. The boat parade was about to begin, and crowds were gathering everywhere beside the harbor. She lost no time in separating herself from her companions. While the Glidewell's were watching the boats sailing in the harbor, Marianne slipped away. She was busy scanning the crowds for a beautiful head of black hair.

Nothing. It was turning into a depressing evening. What was everyone so excited about? Who cared about a bunch of boats with lights floating on some crummy harbor? She walked around aimlessly for about a half hour and decided to go home. It wouldn't be difficult to explain her separation from the Glidewell's. People get lost in crowds.

Heading toward Serpentine Road alone and miserable, she glanced up just in time to see two big smiles on the other side of the road.

"Oh, Hi! I see you were able to get off." Her heart sounded louder than her words.

"Yeah. We decided to see what all the fuss was about." Dave was friendly but not her type. For now, however, Marianne had to accept them as a matched set on one motorcycle.

Tong's eyes pierced her soul, "Would you like to go get a bite to eat?" Would she! He had no idea!

"That would be nice." Cool, calm and collected.

"You're more familiar with Hamilton than we are. Why don't you suggest a place?" Tong reasoned. Was there no end to his good qualities? Generous, reasonable, considerate.

"Let's go to Little Venice. They have good pizza and delicious sandwiches. It's just around the corner."

Moments later they settled into a booth in the small bar and grill in the shadows of the Bermudiana and the Princess hotels. Marianne was in heaven.

"Marianne is a beautiful name. Are you German?" asked Dave.

"Dave, I'm originally from Germany, but I'm American now. I got my Citizenship papers in San Bernardino two years ago."

"Really? I'm from Los Angeles. You don't have to call me Tom or Tong. You can call me Leighton. I guess Flo got you started with that," Leighton said.

Marianne looked into those charming black eyes. "Alright, Leighton." Her heart skipped a beat as she pronounced his name.

It was getting late. Suddenly she realized that she'd better get home soon, or there'd be all kinds of questions. After a short discussion, Leighton decided to take her home. Dave would wait at the Little Venice. Perfect. Ever the gentleman, he drove very carefully. Marianne sat on the passenger seat holding on to the handle to avoid getting too close. He escorted her to the front door. She wondered whether he would try to kiss her goodnight. He didn't.

Walking into the house, Marianne was confused. The signals she was getting were unclear. "*I thought Leighton liked me. Maybe he is already married.*" Maybe he's shy. Maybe. Maybe. She collapsed onto her bed. "*Wow, my life has sure become complicated in just one week*!" Her plan to get him to come to town had worked, but there was no encouragement on his part. What else could she do?

* * *

Dave commented, "Man, she's got eyes for you!"

"You think so?"

"I know so. She hardly noticed that I was sitting in the same booth with both of you."

"She didn't make any moves on the way home, and she mentioned something about her boyfriend, remember?"

"Then why wasn't he with her?"

"I don't know. She sure makes me feel all weird. You think it would be alright for me to ask her out?"

"Sure, why not invite her to go to the beach with us next weekend? If she accepts, you can see how it goes. Stop being so self-conscious about being Chinese."

"Well, I've gone out mostly with Asian girls. This German girl has got me bamboozled." Leighton couldn't quite get used to this new feeling.

"*I think I'll spend more time with her. Maybe my head will clear,*" he thought.

* * *

"Would you like to go to the beach with us next weekend?" Leighton asked as he was bringing an armful of newspapers the next day.

"Us?" She was a little disappointed.

"Yes. Dave and I have plans to go to Elbow Beach. I'm sure he would like to have you come along." Marianne was beginning to become suspicious. Silently she wondered, *"Is he trying to set me up with Dave?"*

"I'd like that. Thanks for the pizza. I had a real good time last night. Tell Dave thanks for letting you take me home on his motorcycle. I'd love to go to Elbow Beach, but his motorcycle isn't big enough for all three of us," she joked.

"We'll take a taxi from your house to the beach and leave the motorcycle in your backyard. Okay?"

"That sounds like fun!"

"What about your boyfriend Bill?"

"Leighton, I'm planning to break up with him. He's known from the start that I was not going to live in Bermuda all my life. We were just boyfriend and girlfriend. Nothing else, and now it's over."

"Okay then. We'll come by at noon on Sunday." Leighton smiled. *"Maybe I have a chance with her, after all."*

* * *

The convertible Bermuda cabs have bright fringed umbrella tops instead of hardtops in the summer. The twenty mile an hour speed limit throughout the islands made their ride to the beach an easy, laugh-filled adventure. The radio was playing "My Prayer" by the Platters. Crowded into the backseat of the small cab, all three hummed along.

A sudden news bulletin on the radio warned of the approaching hurricane, Ione. The eye would pass by Bermuda, but the turbulent seas and capricious winds had already claimed one life. A woman had been swept off a cliff in clear view of her terrified husband. The three looked at each other. Sure, it was windy, but the sun was shining.

“Leighton, let's go anyway. Who knows when we'll get another day off?”

Marianne interrupted, “I agree. We’ll be safe on Elbow Beach which is located in a sheltered cove. There’s no cliff for us to climb on.”

Leighton nodded, and the cab driver mumbled something about crazy Americans, but he didn't refuse to accept the fare for the ride to the beach.

On the beach sand whipped around them, and any hope of swimming was dashed. Yet no one wanted to give up and go home. Dave was determined to brave the wild waves at least once. Towels and blankets had to be anchored down with shoes. Marianne shivered. “Brrr. It’s getting cold.” Three idiots having the time of their lives in a hurricane.

“I’m going to lie down on the blanket to keep it from getting air-borne.” Marianne didn’t want to admit that she was scared of the increasing wind and the roiling ocean. She was cold and hungry. She wrapped herself in a beach towel and lay down. Leighton came over to lie down beside her, draped a towel over her head and put one hand on her shoulder. Suddenly she was filled with a calm warmth that spread all the way to her toes. Marianne dared not peek out from under the towel into Leighton's eyes. She pretended to be resting, but her beating heart drowned out the howling wind.

Dave was yelling something while he was jumping around in the surf, “Hey there you two. Why don't you get in the water?”

“No thanks. We're thinking of heading back home.” Mr. Reasonable.

“Okay, let's go. I don't want to become a statistic anyway.” Dave grumbled as he scrambled out of the water. “I’m hungry. Where is our lunch?”

They huddled together to eat their sandwiches, chatting until the wind got loud enough to drown out their voices.

"This is fun. We ought to come to the beach some time when there's no hurricane."

They laughed and sang all the way home despite the storm clouds which threatened to break at any moment. All the cabbies had rolled up their umbrellas and pulled up the hard tops. The guys were happy and seemed perfectly content to share this date, but Marianne wasn't at all thrilled about this threesome arrangement. "*Who needs Dave?*"

The small Triumph cab dropped them off at Marianne's home. She had already introduced the guys to her folks earlier, so she invited them in for a lemonade before calling it a day.

After their motorcycle roared off, Marianne was still in a happy daze. Tilly surprised Marianne, "Boy, it sure is obvious which one you favor. I don't think it is a good idea for you to see that Chinaman anymore."

There it was. The race thing. The issue.

* * *

Before long it even became obvious to Dave that he was not the one that Marianne wanted to date. Bill also accepted the fact that another man had come between them. Marianne was a goner.

The only one who didn't seem to realize the burning within Marianne was Leighton. Days went by without the slightest move toward intimacy.

On the job in the Terminal BX, he was all business. Pleasant but business. During their free time, things were a bit more relaxed. They ate lunch and worked crossword puzzles together in the terminal cafeteria. They listened to music together. They talked about their interests. They decorated the stationery counter together. They avoided touching each other. Marianne almost exploded with the tension. Something was going to happen even if she herself had to make it happen! She couldn't guess whether Leighton was also feeling the tension.

* * *

Lunchtime had become a pleasant routine for Leighton. Each morning he looked forward to sitting close to this girl in a booth while they were focusing on a crossword puzzle or eating their sandwiches. Even though the cafeteria was usually quite crowded, he was only aware of Marianne. A pleasant joyful feeling seemed to emanate from her presence.

He was pleased to discover that she was not only pretty but also smart as they worked on crossword puzzles in the daily newspaper.

"Why do I feel so weird when I'm around her? Is this what love feels like? I'm going to invite her to go out with me without Dave," he thought. *"I have to find out for myself."*

* * *

"Hey, Edith. My dad is working late today, so I won't be riding with you after work. He'll be by later to drive me home." For the past week, Marianne had been riding home after the store closed with her co-worker, Edith, who lived in the same neighborhood.

"Okay, Marianne. See you tomorrow." As Edith drove off, Marianne got a sinking feeling. "*What if Leighton doesn't stop by today*?" Marianne had learned his usual routine of coming to pick up a newspaper just before the store closed. *"Where is he?"* Moments later, he showed up in civilian clothes.

"Gosh! I'm sure glad to see you. Edith drove off and left me. My dad has already gone home, so now I don't have a ride home.

What am I going to do? A cab is so expensive." She must have looked pitiful.

"All I have is a small motorcycle, but I'd be glad to take you home." Leighton offered. "You're lucky this is my day off." Lucky? No. This was a planned emergency. Marianne had known it was his day off.

"Your motorcycle is fine. You know how to drive very well, and I know you'll get me home safe and sound."

Only two short weeks earlier when he had taken Marianne home from the Little Venice, she had sat way back on the seat and held onto the handle for dear life. This time as the motorcycle roared to life, she put both arms around his waist and gushed, "My life is in your hands." A half hour of bliss.

He responded calmly, "Would you like to go to a movie one of these days?"

"Yes." Yes, yes, yes!

"How about next Saturday night?"

"Yes." Yes, yes, yes!

The ride home was over much too soon.

"Let's sit on the porch for a while. My mom doesn't have dinner ready yet. I'll get us a lemonade." Marianne disappeared into the house while Leighton settled into one of the lounge chairs.

"Here's a refreshing glass of lemonade, Leighton. I was hoping you'd tell me a bit more about your family. You said that you'd just come back from California when we first met."

"Yes, I took a thirty-day leave to go home to Los Angeles. My mother just got out of the hospital last year, so I wanted to visit her."

"Oh? What was wrong? Was she very sick?"

"When I was a little boy, my dad put her in the State Hospital at Norwalk. She was in there for fifteen years."

Marianne was shocked. "State Hospital? Fifteen years? Dang! Why?"

"That's what I've been wondering all those years. Whenever we went to visit her she looked alright, but she just didn't talk to us. I think she missed her little girl."

"You have a sister?"

"Yes, but I don't know her. She was taken to China when she was only three years old, and I was only eight."

"Who took care of you? You had to grow up without your mother?" Marianne still couldn't get over the shock. "I feel so bad for you!"

"It's okay. I had lots of friends and learned to take care of myself. Life's funny like that." Suddenly he looked a bit sad. "Well, I guess I had better head back to the base before it gets dark. See you tomorrow."

Marianne's mind was reeling as he drove off. *"Was his mother insane? What the heck happened? Who is this guy?"*

Inside the house no one suspected a thing. The subterfuge had begun. Still no kiss, however.

* * *

On the way back to the barracks, Leighton thought, *"This girl is someone I could spend my life with. My heart skipped a beat when she told me that her life was in my hands."*

He no longer hesitated to ask her out for the next few months. Thoughts of love and a lifetime together almost pushed the attention to his work aside. Each visit to a beach or a movie made him more certain that he would ask her to marry him some day.

What would she say?

* * *

“Are you still seeing that Chinaman?” John demanded one day.

Marianne responded quietly, “We go to the movies or the beach once in a while. What's wrong with that?”

“I'll tell you what's wrong with it, young lady. The base commander called me in today and told me to stop letting you hang around with that Chinaman. You've been seen all over the base with him.”

“What does the Base Commander have to do with who I date? I still don't see what's wrong with that. I'm over eighteen, and Leighton’s a member of the United States Air Force.”

John got red in the face. “You do what I tell you, young lady!”

Marianne tried to remain calm and logical, but she started to cry. “I don't care about your stupid old base commander. He should take care of his own stupid kids. They're all over the base causing trouble. His daughter is only sixteen and running around with all kinds of different guys.” Her voice got shriller with each word.

“What he does about his kids is beside the point. I’m only concerned with MY kid. This could hurt my Air Force career. You are not to see this guy again. He is not of our race. Don't you realize what you're getting into?”

“He's human and he's better than any of the other guys around here.” Marianne had composed herself. “I can't imagine what this has to do with your career.”

"Come on, Marianne. You're blond and pretty. Don't do this to me." Tilly pleaded. She had been listening to the heated exchange.

"Mutti, you did what you wanted to do even though your mother didn't want you to." Marianne knew how it hurt her mother to be reminded of her heart-wrenching decision to leave Germany and her family, but she had become defensive. Tears were flowing freely.

"Bitte. Lass das doch sein." In moments of stress Tilly always reverted back to German; however, there were no words in any language strong enough to convince Marianne to stop seeing Leighton.

"I'll try." In her heart she knew that trying was useless. Leighton and Marianne had kissed. They had decided to call each other "Love." They had bonded over crossword puzzles together at lunch every other day. They had listened to the Platters singing hits over the loudspeaker together. They had held hands at the movies.

Trying to forget those moments was futile. In order to please her parents, Marianne went out with other guys. She tried, but her heart was no longer free.

* * *

On Christmas Eve 1955, Marianne attended the 10:00 p.m. Mass with Al Falzon. He was a lieutenant and the right race. Her parents approved of him. He was nice, but there was no spark. Al dropped her off around eleven. "Merry Christmas, Al. See you tomorrow." A quick kiss. Blah.

Love stepped out of the shadows. Marianne had told him she'd be home at eleven and to wait for her behind the large oleander tree in front of their house.

The spark! There it was! They fell into each other's embrace. Long tender kisses. Loving whispers.

"If I asked you to marry me, would you say yes?" Leighton asked her under the oleander tree.

"If you asked me I might answer," she teased.

"Would you marry me?" Soft. Loving.

"Oh, Love. I would if I could, but we're not the same race. It's impossible." She couldn't see over the man-made obstacles.

"It's mind over matter." He calmly stated her entire philosophy in that simple phrase. She felt his calm warmth in those words which evoked all her previous experiences. Her mind had already overcome many impossible situations of her precarious life.

"Yes, Love. I would love to be your wife." Yes. Yes. Yes. Yes, Love. "Now I'd better go in. My folks think I went to church with Al Falzon. They have no idea that I had a date with you after church."

"It's too bad that your folks are giving you a hard time. I like your dad. We're in the same squadron."

"Love, I'm sure they'll be okay once I tell them that I intend to marry you." Marianne was sure her mother would understand, but she kept her fingers crossed about her stepfather. "We'll cross that bridge when we come to it. Let's talk about it tomorrow. Goodnight and Merry Christmas, my sweet Leighton Tong."

* * *

Triplett was still awake when Leighton returned to the barracks. "Hey, why so late? It's Christmas. You must have had a heavy date. Still going with that German girl?"

Leighton seemed to be in a daze. "Yeah."

“What’s wrong with you, guy?”

“Absolutely nothing. I proposed and she accepted.”

“You’re kidding!” Triplett’s voice woke up the guy in a near-by bunk.

“Keep it down, guys. I’m trying to get some sleep. It’s Christmas for cryin’ out loud!”

“Sorry! But my friend here is getting married! That’s something to shout about.”

“Congratulations! Now good night!” the guy grumbled and turned over.”

Leighton didn’t get much sleep that night.

* * *

“That's a man's prerogative!!!” John was livid when Marianne told him about her acceptance of Leighton’s marriage proposal.

In their argument about interracial marriages and the social problems of the resulting children, Marianne had just pointed to the fact that American servicemen had brought lots of Japanese and Korean wives to America and that their children could become the spouses of any children Leighton and she would have.

“If you insist on going through with this marriage, we'll disown you!” roared John.

Tilly ran crying to her bedroom to cry because Marianne screamed, “Leighton is worth a lot more than I could ever inherit from a poor Air Force sergeant!” Ouch!

* * *

So here was the challenge: If Marianne married her beloved Leighton, she would be disinherited. This thought did not scare her. Marianne's perspective on what she might inherit from her parents was greatly affected by the events she had already witnessed. After the war she had seen plenty of people start over from nothing. Some people had lost everything they had, and yet they thrived. There was nothing to inherit from John, anyway. He had been unable to pay for her college; instead, he had told her to make a man happy. Marianne was certain that her wonderful Leighton would provide a secure future for her. The thought that she might lose her mother's love, however, was like a sword through her heart.

"Mutti, Leighton and I want to get married in May. Do you think you could make me a wedding dress?"

"Marianne, you know that I left my mother for love. It's been very difficult for me. This marriage will be very difficult for you. I don't want to fight with you. If you really love your Leighton, I won't be able to stop it."

"He's a very special person, Mutti. I'm truly in love with him."

"Alright. We'll go shopping next week for some material and a pattern, and I'll sew a beautiful bridal gown for you, but you'll have to make all the other arrangements yourself. Daddy and I still don't approve, you know."

On Valentine's Day, Leighton surprised Marianne with an engagement ring. Their wedding plans were simple. There was a chapel on Kindley Air Force Base. The reception could take place at the NCO Club. It would be a small ceremony with just a few friends.

* * *

Marianne no longer accepted dates with any other guys. Leighton had become the center of her universe. His motorcycle managed to carry them to various hideaways throughout the Bermuda Isles.

One such place was Buckey's Deli in Paget. The hot dogs with spicy piccalilli relish were worth the half hour ride. "Let's go to Buckey's for a hot dog," was one of Marianne's favorite suggestions. Late one spring afternoon, the weather turned from sunny to stormy and cold while they were sitting in the restaurant.

"What are we going to do now?" wondered Marianne.

Leighton said, "We could wait for a while. Maybe it will clear up."

An hour later it was still storming and getting dark. "We need to get home, Love. My mother will have a cow if I don't turn up soon."

"Okay, let's just go." The guy behind the counter shook his head.

The wind and rain had let up a little, but it was still very uncomfortable. "Man, I hope we don't get pneumonia riding in this mess for a half hour."

"I have a thick Air Force blanket in my saddle bag. We can use it to shield us from the wind. I'm also wearing my coat backwards, and you can keep warm behind me."

For twenty minutes, they rode through the dark windy rain until they reached the Longbird Bridge near Kindley Air Base. Suddenly, the motorcycle made a terrible noise and stopped. "What in the world just happened?"

Leighton took a flashlight out of the saddlebag. "Damn it! The chain broke! There's no way I can fix this here. I hope a taxi will come along soon."

For a little while they held each other close under the blanket. "Boy, this is one night I'll be glad to get home," laughed Marianne.

"Hey, I see some headlights! Let's hope it's a cab. Yup! He's stopping!"

Leighton and Marianne climbed gratefully into the cab, "First take my girl home, and then you can drop me off at the barracks on base."

"Yes sir!"

* * *

"Gosh, I'm glad we have beautiful weather today. How did you get your motorcycle back?"

"Dave and I went to pick it up. I fixed the chain. There wasn't any other damage."

"You mean that we can ride to our favorite little hideaway in Somerset this afternoon?"

"Yes, let's leave right after work."

"I don't think it will storm today," Leighton predicted as he parked the motorcycle near one of Bermuda's beautiful white-roofed homes.

Marianne's heart was beating faster as they approached the tiny pier on foot. No one seemed to notice them. Located on a large private estate, the wooden pier over a shallow tide pool was more decorative than practical. There was no fence. Over the years, other couples must have embraced on these boards and enjoyed the view of the coral reefs jutting out of the vast ocean. "It's our turn," said Marianne.

Sitting quietly side by side, they were overwhelmed with their love for each other. A soft kiss. A gentle hand reached under her blouse. She shivered. Another soft kiss. Time stood still until his wallet fell out of his pocket into the water.

"*Good thing! I was about to give in*," thought Marianne. She said, "Quick, Love! Grab it before it floats away."

Leighton had already removed his shoes, so he jumped into the shallow water to retrieve the wallet. "Well, I guess I'll have to get a new ID card and driver's license."

The passionate moment had passed.

* * *

A couple of weeks later Leighton and Marianne were wrapped in a blanket on Horseshoe Beach. Their bathing suits didn't prevent the passionate embrace. Leighton's hands were no longer shy. He whispered, "Your skin is so soft that I can hardly breathe."

Her breasts quivered with each touch. "Oh, Love! I want you so much, but I'm afraid.

"What are you afraid of, my sweet Marianne?" he whispered close to her ear as he ran his fingers through her hair.

"Love, I love you and I want you but I'm afraid of getting pregnant."

He gently stroked her belly, "I would love to have a baby with you."

Her hand reached out to the bulge in his bathing suit. As it grew, she moved her other hand to his chest to make him breathe even harder.

"We can't, my sweet Love. Our relationship is difficult enough without taking a chance on having a baby before we're married."

"It's alright, Love. You're making me feel so very good. That is what's important for now. We have a lifetime to make up for waiting." Mr. Reasonable. Always so considerate.

Marianne threw the blanket back. "Let's go in the water to cool off. Last one in is a rotten egg," she yelled as she jumped into the waves.

* * *

"There's a movie I'd like to see, Love."

"Oh? Which one?" asked Leighton.

"Jennifer Jones and William Holden are starring in 'Love is a Many-Splendored Thing.' I've heard the theme song on the radio, and I really want to see the movie."

Afterwards, Marianne cried on Leighton's shoulder. "This movie really touched my heart. My parents are starting to give me a lot of trouble about being engaged to you. I don't know whether they will give me permission to marry you or not. I didn't even know about the Bermudian law that parents have to give permission if the bride is under twenty-one. I'm glad you've never been married before, or that would give me even more to worry about. You know I'm Catholic, and it's a sin to marry a divorced person."

"I thought you told me that your mother was divorced."

"She is, and so is my stepfather. That's what makes me so confused when they are all upset with me loving a perfectly wonderful eligible man."

"It's because I'm Chinese, isn't it?"

"Yes, my mother is mellow about it, but my Dad is very prejudiced. He's got her under control."

* * *

"But, Mutti, I need your approval and permission to get married here in Bermuda because I'm not twenty-one yet. Besides, I love you, and don't want to fight with you."

"Sorry, Marianne. I've changed my mind. If you insist on going through with this marriage, you'll have to do it without me. I can't do this to Daddy."

How often had Marianne heard this disclaimer throughout her life in America? Tilly had left her own parents, her country, and, in fact, her daughter behind to please this man. Her explanation for her decisions included that he was taking them to America where freedom and opportunity would make their lives into heaven on Earth. Daddy had continually promoted the virtues of the human rights that people enjoyed under American laws. Unlike other countries, America valued human life. Marianne was convinced; however, when she found the man she wanted to marry, her stepfather had set those values aside. As time went on, Marianne became painfully aware of Daddy's hypocritical bigotry while Mutti was blinded by her love for her "rescuer" from her war-torn marriage and country.

* * *

By her nineteenth birthday in May, Marianne had made up her mind to leave Bermuda. The atmosphere had become more and more intolerable. Her heart could no longer endure being alternately subjected to vitriolic arguments and passionate encounters.

"I got an offer from Tante Leni to come stay with her and her husband," Marianne showed the letter to her mother. "I also got a very nasty letter from Daddy's parents. They told me that I would always have to live in slums if I married a Chinaman."

"Marianne, I wrote to everybody in the family about the mistake you are making. I asked them to write to you."

"Why haven't people learned that prejudice causes death and destruction? Look what happened to Germany!"

Tilly went loudly on the defensive, "You don't know anything about that, Marianne! Stop throwing those kinds of arguments in my face. Daddy and I don't want you to marry Leighton, and that is that!"

Rather than fight with her parents, Marianne decided to take up her aunt's offer to come live with her until Tilly and John got transferred. Leni had gotten married and lived in a beautiful Southern California home. Marianne appreciated her compassion in her letters even though she suspected Leni would try to talk her out of the relationship with Leighton.

A tearful good-bye just three days before the date they had originally set as their wedding day, closed one chapter of her life. Marianne would never again feel the unconditional child-like love for her mother. Alone and penniless, this resourceful woman had nurtured the little girl through unimaginable difficulties. Now she turned her back on that same girl, deprived her of her love and supported the man who had become an adversary.

* * *

"Let's write each other every day, Love."

"I'll miss you a lot, but letters might help."

Neither one was certain that letters would do any good. Would they ever meet again? Would they find someone else? The plane was waiting on the tarmac to carry Marianne away.

In the Museum

"Randy! It's good to see you again."

"Hey Joe!"

"Did you come to find out whether they ever got together again?"

"Once a girl goes away, it usually over."

"You still think so with all you've learned about Marianne?"

"Hey, she was nineteen and pretty. Who knows what'll happen in California?"

"I know what happened there. Do you want to hear?"

"Sure, but what I'd really like to know is how you know so much about history."

"I lived it Randy; I still live it."

1956 Leighton

Dave and Triplett noticed Leighton's unhappy face.

"You want to talk about it, Leighton?"

"No, there's nothing to talk about. She left. I guess her parents got to her." He averted his face to hide the tears rolling down his cheeks.

"Hey, there are lots of nice girls in the world. You'll find another one."

"You're no help, Trip," shrugged Leighton. "I really thought Marianne and I had something going. Who knows whether we'll ever see each other again."

"Come on, let's drown our sorrows in a couple of beers at the NCO Club."

1956 Marianne

This time, Marianne had no mental conflicts about writing. At the end of each day, loving words flowed freely onto the paper, expressing her thoughts and feelings with ease. At last, she discovered the power of words that she had long considered a forbidden mystery. Her world opened up, and though she didn't write much besides the letters to Leighton, she no longer felt the resentment previously associated with writing. She even wrote her mother and grandmother now and then.

Daily letters continued to fly across the Atlantic to keep Leighton and Marianne in touch. Aunt Leni tried her best to help her forget him, but Marianne's heart just wasn't ready to give up her true love.

Being very much aware that she was only a nineteen year old girl, Marianne wasn't completely convinced that the rest of the world was wrong about Leighton. For the moment, she was willing to go along with the ideas of others. Leni introduced her to a young man who would have pleased the entire family as an appropriate mate. "He's my friend's son. I think you'll like him, and he has a nice car."

Rudy had graduated from Cal Tech with a degree in Electrical Engineering and was working at JPL (Jet Propulsion Laboratory). He had all the blond qualifications, except that Marianne didn't love him. She let him take her to fancy restaurants, the State Fair in Pomona, to San Juan Capistrano, to Big Bear and various other places.

"Rudi, I hope you don't mind that I'm still wearing my engagement ring."

"I don't mind, Marianne, but I keep hoping that you'll forget him and start thinking about me."

"I like you Rudy, and I'm really grateful for your generosity. I have fun with you, but my heart is not free."

"Well, we're both very young. Perhaps in time…."

* * *

One day in October Marianne received a letter from Los Angeles with an unfamiliar handwriting. "*What is this? Allen Tong?*" she wondered.

Dear Marianne,

My brother Leighton has told us about you. He gave me your address and suggested that we get together some time.

My wife Rose and I would love to invite you and show you around Hollywood. Please call me at 555-4300 to make arrangements for us to pick you up.

Best Wishes, Allen Tong

"*I can't believe it! Leighton told his brother about me*." She thought while dialing the phone that same afternoon. "What a pleasant surprise! It's so good to hear from a member of Leighton's family. Thank you for inviting me."

"Rose and I will come to pick you up on Sunday morning. We'll make a nice day of it and have you back in Covina in plenty of time to get some rest before going back to work on Monday morning."

"That will be wonderful. I'm looking forward to meeting you."

Marianne was surprised to discover that Rose was blond. She was of Polish descent and met Allen on a tennis court after he had gotten back from Korea. He was playing tennis for the Marines and participated in Toys for Tots. Rose was the secretary for Toys for Tots. "My family is very upset with me, Rose. Is your family okay with your marriage?" asked Marianne.

"Yes, they are now. It was a little awkward at first."

Allen changed the subject, "We're going to drive over to Hollywood. Have you ever heard of Grauman's Chinese Theater?"

"No."

"It's one of the most famous movie theaters in Hollywood. We have tickets for "Cinerama Holiday." We thought you might enjoy it."

"Wow! Thank you Allen."

"Afterward we'll have dinner at Lawry's restaurant on La Cienega Boulevard in Beverly Hills. It's a very famous place."

Marianne truly appreciated how Leighton's brother and his wife treated her. On the way home she expressed her gratitude.

"Allen, your brother told me quite a bit about how you and he practically raised yourselves. I'm so sorry about that, and I'm glad that your mother is home again."

"Thank you, Marianne."

"No, Allen. Thank YOU! This has been a truly memorable day."

* * *

"Long Distance phone call from Bermuda for you, Marianne. You can take it in the office." she had been working at the Magan Clinic in Covina for six months. Her heart had been broken in Bermuda, but she was healing. Leni and her husband Jack were kind hosts, so she felt comfortable in their home. The passionate romance in Bermuda had gradually become a steady flame of real love and affection.

"Who could be calling from Bermuda? Is Mutti calling?" When she recognized Leighton's voice, she cried for two expensive minutes. Overseas long distance charges were no joke.

He finally said, "Love, this call is costing $8 a minute. Please stop crying so we can talk. I called to find out whether you want me to come to California to get married, or whether we should break up. I can't go on like this."

"Yes! Come! We can get married in Los Angeles." Marianne had been ready to get married in Bermuda, but Bermudian law had been an unsurmountable obstacle. In California there was no such restriction.

"Ok then, I'll be there in two weeks. I'll pick you up at the Magan Clinic on Monday after work." With promises of undying love, they ended their expensive conversation.

* * *

"You're going to Germany with us!" Tilly insisted. John's tour of duty in Bermuda was over. His new Air Force orders were for Ramstein Air Base in Germany. They had come to California to persuade Marianne to move to Germany with them. It would be the perfect opportunity to find a proper German husband for Marianne.

Half-hearted Marianne had let her mother buy her a warm winter coat and obtain a visa to travel to Germany on her passport. Her mind still vacillated, but she was eagerly waiting for Leighton. She would be able to think more clearly once she saw him again in person.

Eventually, she realized that she could not continue to please all the people she loved. No matter what she decided, someone was going to get hurt. One thing she was sure of: it wasn't going to be herself.

As a child she had cooperated with parents who were no longer married to each other. For five years she had obediently lived with her grandparents. She had been an obedient daughter, braving an ocean voyage to be with her mother. For the following five years she had accepted the rather bigoted ideas of a German-born American step-father. Several times in her young life, circumstances had forced her to be courageous beyond her years. She had already survived serious illnesses in the midst of a war, traveled unaccompanied, and fought for her rights in a foreign language. She would have preferred to be supported by her parents instead of fighting for her life, but here she was, standing up for her own heart again.

"Leighton is coming, and we're planning to get married here in California." She tried to be matter-of-fact, but she was going against her habit of deferring to her parents. "I know that you won't be happy about that, but sooner or later I will have to become an adult."

"Be reasonable, Marianne," her mother implored.

* * *

Leighton borrowed a car from one of his friends to meet Marianne after work. He was nervous about how she would react to his showing up at the Magan Clinic. Her letters had been very encouraging, but one never knew. "*Girls are so fickle*."

She had agreed to get married in Los Angeles, but would she keep her word?

The front door of the Magan Clinic opened, and Marianne stepped out. All of Leighton's doubts washed away in a flood of relief. She noticed him, flashed a brilliant smile and ran toward him.

"It's so good to be together again! Let's go to Las Vegas for the weekend." Leighton suggested after a lengthy embrace.

"Las Vegas? I'm not old enough to gamble," answered Marianne.

"You're gambling right now," he laughed.

"That's true," she agreed.

* * *

After work on Friday, Leighton came to pick her up in another borrowed car. "We'll leave for Las Vegas after we have a bite to eat." I have to return this car to Marlowe on Sunday afternoon."

"Let me go pick up a couple of things at my aunt's house. I really should let my folks know where I'm going and that I won't be going to Germany with them."

"Okay, we can do that. My friends have been letting me borrow their cars. Haven't you noticed that I drove a different car every time I came to Covina this week?"

"Yes, I noticed, but mostly I noticed you, my handsome husband-to-be!" Marianne bubbled.

A few hours later they were heading East on Highway 66. "Let's stop in Barstow for the night. We're both tired, and Las Vegas is still a long drive on Highway 15."

"Okay." Marianne was apprehensive. This would be their first night in a bed together.

The neon sign in front of Motel "Lucky Seven" blinked "Vacancy." Confidently, Leighton parked the car and went to register as Mr. and Mrs. Tong.

"But we're not married yet," whispered Marianne with a smile.

"We'll be married next Saturday. That's close enough for government work," laughed Leighton.

"You want to get some snacks in the store over there? Then we can relax and listen to some music. I noticed a radio in the room."

"Good idea. I'm hungry again," agreed Leighton.

* * *

"Hey this radio is coin-operated. Every fifteen minutes you have to put in another quarter. That's kind of expensive for poor people like us."

"Watch me." Leighton went out to the car and got the First Aid kit out of the trunk.

"What do you need that for?" wondered Marianne.

"See this adhesive tape? Here is a quarter. The tape will let me lower the quarter into the slot, and the radio turns on. As soon as the radio turns off, I can pull it out and lower it again for another fifteen minutes."

"Clever!" admired Marianne.

After getting ready for bed in the locked bathroom, Marianne, wearing a long nightgown, got into bed and pulled the blanket all the way to her neck. Leighton got the message that not much was going to happen. He kept his T-shirt and underwear on and got into bed beside her. Their hands explored their pulsating bodies lying within inches of each other. Listening to Doris Day's "Que Sera, Sera," the lovers exchanged intimate kisses, but neither one made the move to quench their thirst for each other before they dozed off in embrace.

The morning noises of the motel woke them up. Still locked in each other's arms they gave in to their passion. "Oh Love! That was unbelievable!" In a daze, Marianne went through the motions of brushing her teeth and getting dressed.

Leighton floated to the car carrying their overnight bags. He looked back through the open door at Marianne standing in the room. With a big smile, she was pointing at the bed. He stepped back into the room and shut the door. "Let's do it again," he whispered. She yielded to his love as their bodies joined once more in the rhythm of life.

* * *

After a weekend of passion in a Las Vegas motel and a few short visits to a couple of Casinos they returned to Covina. Leighton dropped Marianne off because she still had to work another week. "Where have you been?" demanded her mother.

"We've been to Las Vegas. Next Saturday we're getting married in Los Angeles, and the week after that I'm going back to Bermuda with Leighton."

Tilly was speechless. She turned and walked into another room.

* * *

Marianne had taken Wednesday afternoon off. Tilly noticed how nervously Marianne kept looking out the front window. "What's going on? How come you're not at work?"

Marianne answered, "I'm waiting for Leighton to pick me up. Finally Leighton drovc up in another borrowed car. "There he is, and I'm going with him. We are going to a Justice of Peace to get our marriage license. I'd love to have you come. We'll wait if you want to get ready," She almost begged her mother.

"No, Marianne, I am not going to be at your wedding. This is completely your own doing."

"Mutti, he's come to pick me up. I'm leaving. Please come with us to our wedding next Saturday." Marianne was very sad because she realized that her mother was adamant. Again there was crying.

Leni and Tilly hugged her and tried to cajole her into another decision. "Don't go, please." John got loud and physical. He knocked Marianne onto a couch and kicked her in the behind. Leni's husband Jack came storming into the room, "Leave the girl alone!"

Marianne ran out of the house with her mother chasing after her. Tilly was still sobbing as she was begging Leighton to be sensible. "Please don't do this." She tried to reason with him, "Think of the children. Think about what you're doing!"

Leighton was dumbfounded. "Children?" He looked at Marianne, "What do you want, Love?"

"Let's go!"

They drove off. Somewhere the sound of breaking glass reminded Marianne of the hearts that were breaking.

The clerk at the courthouse looked at Leighton and then turned to Marianne and asked, "Do your parents know what you're doing?"

"Yes."

The lady nodded. She felt that had done her duty and handed Marianne the marriage license. "That will be ten dollars, please."

On Saturday Benny and Norman were the only witnesses at their small wedding at a chapel on Olympia Avenue.

* * *

The next day, Marianne and Leighton were surprised by about twenty of Leighton's friends who had arranged a reception for the newlyweds at Tate's restaurant in Los Angeles.

* * *

"I want my parents to meet you," said Leighton after the reception. "Are you ready to meet them?"

"Yes, I'd love to meet them. I've met your friends, and I've already met Allen and Rose. They have really welcomed me. I'm sorry that my parents have been so nasty to you."

Leighton smiled, "Well, my dad did say something about some nice Chinese girls living in the neighborhood when I told him about you, but I ignored him. I'm sure he'll be mellow."

Both Leighton's mother and Marianne were very shy about meeting each other, but there were no hard feelings. Even Uncle George and his wife welcomed Marianne to the dinner they had prepared for the occasion. Leighton's brother Gene had been discharged from the military, so he also met and welcomed

Marianne. Jerry, the youngest, had joined the Air Force right after he graduated the year before. He was stationed in Missouri, so he couldn't come.

"Thank you for your hospitality. I love your son," Marianne said as she hugged Leighton's mother. The language barrier made any further conversation impossible. They may not have understood the words, but they both sensed the good intentions.

* * *

"Boy, oh boy! How poor we are! You've spent all your savings on this trip, and I don't have anything saved up. What are we going to do in Bermuda till the next payday? Where are we going to live?"

"I told my roommate to look for an apartment while I was gone. He knows we we're getting married and would need a place. He's a good friend and I'm sure he'll have something ready for us. Don't worry about a thing. You have a husband now!"

"You're right! And you have a wife!" added Marianne.

"Did you know that the Air Force will let us stay in Bermuda for another year and a half? Single people only get to stay a year and a half, but married people get to stay three years."

"Yes, that's why my parents were stationed there for three years. I'm so happy to go back to a familiar place. I've moved around far too much in my life."

Leighton gave her a big hug, "Love, from now on we'll always have each other, no matter where we live."

"Oh Love! You make me so happy," said Marianne as she nestled into his loving embrace.

* * *

Leighton and Marianne rented a motel room in Los Angeles for the following week. He had to borrow a car from friends to drop Marianne off at the Magan Clinic each morning, return the car and borrow another car from another friend to pick her up after work.

For lunch Marianne usually walked alone to a small diner in Covina to grab a sandwich. Just as she was going to lunch on her last day of work, her mother suddenly appeared in front of her.

"Well, hello, Mrs. Tong." Tilly smiled and hugged Marianne, "I knew you'd do it. Let's go have some lunch."

Marianne kissed her mother. "I'll have a hamburger," she smiled.

The Epilogue

Memories

Be kind, O spirits, as the soul explores
The Caverns haunted by its familiars.
It is the time. Marianne must speak.
Grant her the strength to bring this opus to fruition.
Guide the eye through the terrible light
And let it not be blinded by the awesome dark.
As memories crowd memories, and visions blur the sight,
One shape appears to take control of life: Leighton.
Under the Oleander tree, Love grows.
There is no Triangle over Bermuda when
War-weary meets Street-wise. Nothing had prepared them
For the filmy, incredibly soft,
Absolute.

Airplanes with bombs disappeared.
Crowds of skeletons disappeared.
All threats were obliterated and replaced
With the petals of Easter lilies and sweet odors
Of Hibiscus, Herculean muscles, and Heaven on Earth!
Inevitably, bliss is not blessed by all.
Prejudice, jealousy, prejudice, hate, prejudice, despair...
At every turn, the fragile embryo of new love meets
Opposition!

Has not one soul compassion for two young lovers?
Stolen moments on pink beaches; a shy hand held
In the enveloping charm of a movie theater;
Brief floating on a dance floor before the parting.
As the great machine lifts off, a final tear
Dissolves their gaze. Each is alone and vulnerable
Again.

Above the clouds, Love is propelled toward the West.
On the ground, Love slouches toward a sleepless night.
The world rejoices. Miscegenation has been thwarted
At the expense of two young hearts.

Yet love does not die. As with the wings of angels,
The great machines made by man float daily missives
Between Marianne and Leighton.

A new wonder appears: the magic of words.
Songs of longing and verses of desire make daily
Voyages across the continent.
Each soothing line erases another tear.
Each written thought strengthens their resolve:
No power on Earth would destroy their precious hope.
Time, space, and opposition would be vanquished.

Had not the world failed to dampen their childhood?
Had not two broken children grown to meet and love?
Has not the human spirit strength to transcend the wall?
There will be music; there will be light; there will be

Living Love!

The following pictures are from the author's personal collection, her husband's personal collection, or from the Wikipedia Commons used with permission.

Marianne with her mother, Tilly

Marianne with her father, Jakob

Jakob during the war

Suey Ping with her three oldest children, Allen, Leighton and Eugene

Jack with his four sons, Allen, Eugene, Jerome and Leighton

Leighton in Junior High

After the war, U. S. Army soldiers were ordered to take pictures of the destruction. One of these ruins was the apartment house where Marianne lived.

Tilly with Marianne and Lotte with Helga before they escaped to St. Wolfgang together

This is the house in Macken where Marianne found a home with her grandparents after the war

Marianne loved watching the old ladies of the village spinning wool from fleece

Martha, Marianne's best friend in Macken

A typical small estate in Hunsrück villages

Vintage furnishings from Leighton and Marianne's youth

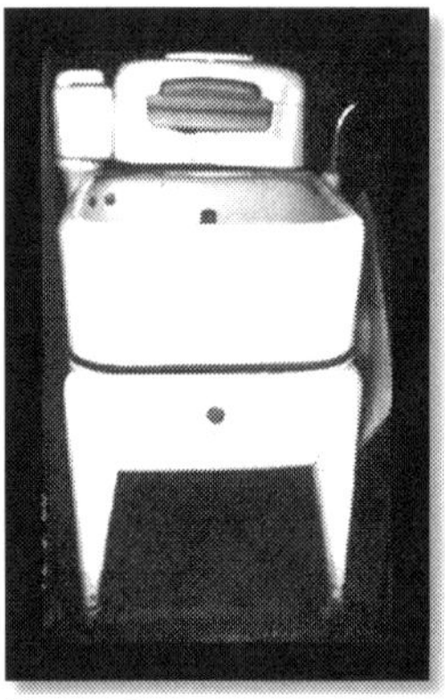

Figure 5wringer washer

Figure 5Kitchen stove

Figure 5Free-standing kitchen cabinet

Figure 5Free-standing heater

Figure 5Table-top radio

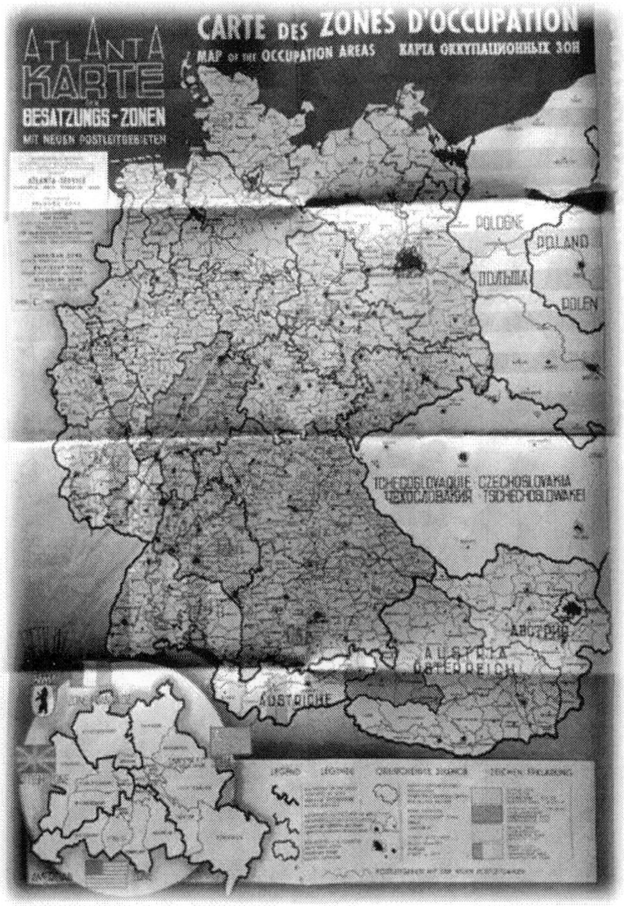

The map (from the personal collection of Marianne's father) shows the four occupation zones. After the war, the Allies divided up Germany which no longer had an autonomous German government. While the Soviet Union claimed the Eastern Part of Germany and a part of Berlin, the other three zones were occupied by Britain, France and the U.S. The Germans jokingly referred to these three zones as "Trizonesien."

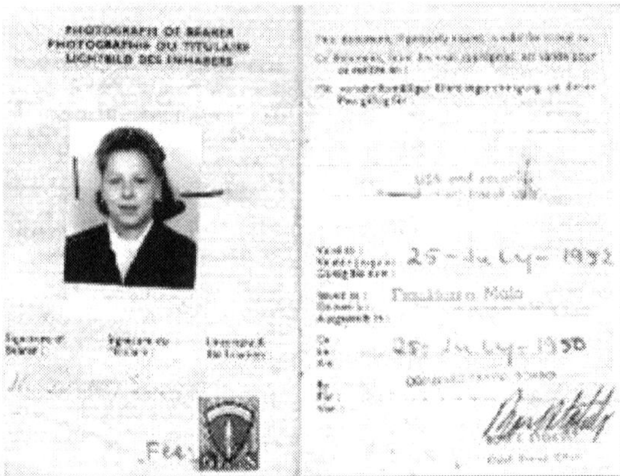

Marianne's Passport

The ship SS Italia that safely brought Marianne to America

Marianne's first Christmas in America with new grandparents

New American friend, Janice

The hated typewriter

Leighton makes friends in San Antonio

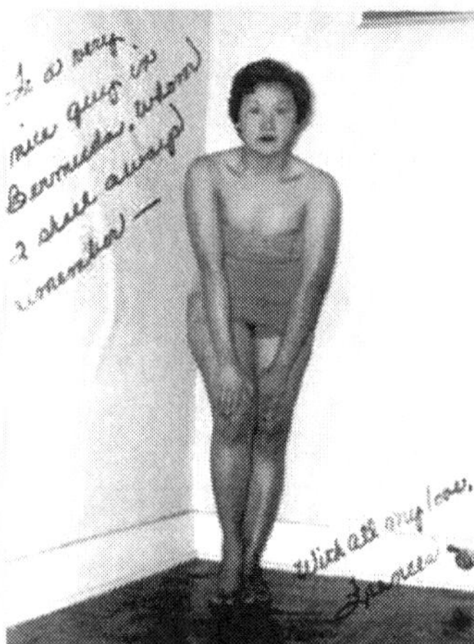

Frances, Leighton's girlfriend

Bill, Marianne's boyfriend

Graduation from Mount Saint Agnes

Marianne on her motorized bike

Leighton with his motorcycle

Leighton

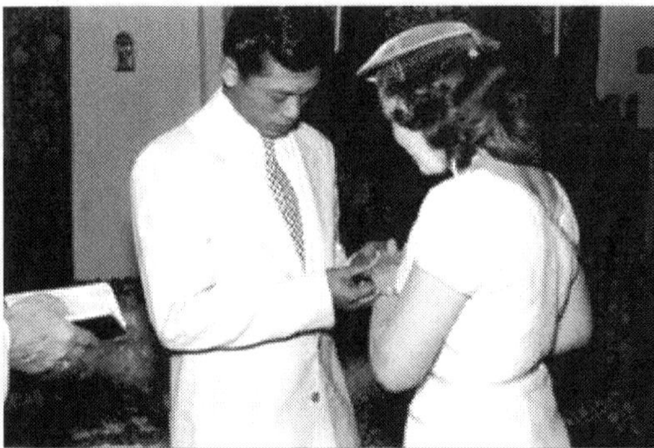

The Wedding

The Reception

About the Author

Simon Miller is the author's pseudonym. She lives in Northern California with her husband.

Books by Marianne Tong

The Little Girl That Could, a Memoir

Mindpieces, a Collection of Short Works

Banking, Bowling and Beethoven, A grandmother's story

Maria Lives! A woman of courage (bilingual English/German)

Children's books (English, Spanish and German versions)

A New Home for Marianne

Marianne Makes a Difficult Decision

Marianne's Journey

Acknowledgements and Sources:

I want to express my gratitude to my husband for sharing his personal pictures, memories and journals. His continual support of this project proved to be invaluable.

Critical reading and editing are an essential part of any literary endeavor. I want to thank my daughters, Vivienne Powell and Kathryn Rogers for their honest comments, insightful suggestions and expert proof-reading.

In gathering the materials for this novel, I used the following:

Personal photos and journals of Leighton Tong

Personal collection of photos and maps of Jakob Simon

Personal photos from the collection of Marianne Tong

Some information and text from Wikipedia with permission

Marianne Simon Miller Tong

Manufactured by Amazon.ca
Bolton, ON

29482441R00146